A WOMAN OF MANY USES

The roaming gypsy band that had raised Pilar
used her to dazzle strangers with her dancing and
leave them ripe for plunder.

The imperious aristocrat who wed Pilar used her
to shock the polite society he hated—and to
spark the interest of the lady he lusted for.

The infamous scoundrel who learned the secret
of Pilar's birth used her as the instrument of his
proud brother's ruination.

So many shameless people used Pilar in so many
scandalous ways . . .

. . . but as all of them were to learn, making a
plaything of Pilar was playing with fire. . . .

LORD GILMORE'S BRIDE

Lord Gilmore's Bride

by

Sheila Walsh

(formerly titled: *A Fine Silk Purse*)

A SIGNET BOOK

NEW AMERICAN LIBRARY

TIMES MIRROR

NAL BOOKS ARE ALSO AVAILABLE AT DISCOUNTS IN BULK
QUANTITY FOR INDUSTRIAL OR SALES-PROMOTIONAL USE.
FOR DETAILS, WRITE TO PREMIUM MARKETING DIVISION,
NEW AMERICAN LIBRARY, INC., 1301 AVENUE OF THE
AMERICAS, NEW YORK, NEW YORK 10019.

Published by arrangement with
Hutchinson Publishing Group, Ltd.

SIGNET TRADEMARK REG. U.S. PAT. OFF. AND FOREIGN COUNTRIES
REGISTERED TRADEMARK—MARCA REGISTRADA
HECHO EN CHICAGO, U.S.A.

SIGNET, SIGNET CLASSICS, MENTOR, PLUME and MERIDIAN BOOKS
are published by The New American Library, Inc.,
1301 Avenue of the Americas, New York, New York 10019

First Signet Printing, April, 1979

1 2 3 4 5 6 7 8 9

PRINTED IN THE UNITED STATES OF AMERICA

1

A harvest moon sailed full and clear above the trees, chasing the wind and flooding the rugged terrain with cold silver light laced with black, inpenetrable shadows.

Three horsemen breasted the rise which marked the boundary of Gilmore land and reined in, the central figure swaying forward lightly in his saddle. His arm lifted in a wide sweep to encompass the near distance where a cluster of roofs, polished to a dull pewter sheen, nestled snugly under the protective mantle of a tall-steepled church.

The moon's light picked out a crisp fall of lace at the wrist, a shimmer of silver tissue like frosting beneath the dark coat.

"There, Ham—what did I tell you? A clear run ... best part of a mile and straight as you please! Nothing to it barring a few trifling hedges. I'll lay you a pony I make it to the church before either of you!"

The words hung unchallenged on the clear night air. Impatience sharpened the deep, resonant drawl. "Well? What do you say?"

Sir Roger Hammell urged his mount alongside. A splendidly curled, powdered toupee surmounted a pleasant face, curiously at odds with the painted image which fashion demanded he should present.

"If you must know, dear boy," he retorted with the brutal candor of the true friend, "I say you'd have done better not to broach that last bottle of Pocklington's port. It's my belief it was corked!"

"And has addled my wits? Well, you're wrong, my dear, but it don't signify. Drunk or sober, I can steer a straight course—my father covered that ground regularly and he was never more than three parts sober that I ever heard in all his days."

"Aye . . . and put paid to a rakehell existence riding recklessly to hounds," finished Sir Roger, unimpressed. " 'Tis an example I have no wish to emulate, I thank you!"

Theodore Maximilian Augustus, Sixth Viscount Gilmore, uttered a snort of disgust and swung around. "And Adam, my worthy cousin?"

"Is desolated to disappoint you, boy, but he would as lief not risk a broken leg or worse in order to prove himself the equal of your reprehensible parent." This man was older than the other two—and noticeably less fashionable in his dress. There was a touch of whimsical humor in the quiet voice.

"Well, I call you a damned chicken-hearted pair!"

"Oh, come now," Adam Carvray urged. "You'd not really make a race of it—at night—and with Ham none too sure of the ground?"

"Curse you, Adam," the Viscount drawled softly. "Why must you always spoil sport? Did you know they call you Gilmore's conscience?"

"Perhaps Gilmore is in need of a conscience," said Adam quietly, refusing to rise to the insult.

His cousin was shamed into a half-angry laugh. He spurred his horse. "Oh, very well. No race. But I mean to ride that way, nonetheless. You may both do as you please, but I am too confoundedly restless to seek my bed."

His mood communicated itself to his hunter—a high-couraged, but nervy creature. The gelding flattened its ears, lost vital concentration, and skidded, setting a small avalanche of stones rattling into the darkness down the narrow, tortuous path.

"Restless!" groaned Sir Roger, setting off in pursuit. "Bless me if I ever knew such a jumpy creature! Always on the go! You'll not believe this, Carvray," he called over his shoulder, "but having lured me all the way up here into Yorkshire, what have we done these past three days? Tramped the grouse moors in a damned mizzle!"

"I thought that was why you came," Theo retorted. "To shoot grouse."

"So I did, dear boy, so I did . . . but I confess I had hoped for something more—an orgy or two, perhaps? Instead, we must needs ride miles every night to some plaguey dull card party. Not a fair Paphian in sight! Not even your delectable Suzanne."

"Mrs. Verney has gone to Paris," Theo said shortly.

"It's true, then? Didn't care to mention it before we left Town . . . rumor had it you two had quarreled . . . over the Lady Eustacie."

"You shouldn't pay heed to *on-dits*, Ham! Suzanne is visiting a sick aunt."

"As you say, dear boy. Incidentally, what *are* you going to do about the deplorable Eustacie?"

"Nothing."

Adam Carvray was a mild-mannered man, yet listening he felt sorely tempted to wash his hands of his volatile young cousin. Theo was a free agent, after all, Adam's only concern being the management of his estates—a task he had undertaken for Theo's father in gratitude for his patronage—a task he enjoyed and was content to continue. It was not his affair if Theo chose to set the world at odds.

Except, of course, that he loved Theo—had loved him from those very first hours, seeing the tiny flailing fists already thrusting upward in defiance of the nurserymaid's attempts to confine him in swaddling bands.

Perhaps if his mother had lived—or if his father had been less of a profligate—Theo would have grown to manhood less wild. Instead, the Fifth Viscount had married again, and Gertrude Shenton was a social-climbing heiress who had shown no interest in the already lively small boy entrusted to her care.

It was left to Adam, therefore, to be father, mother, brother, and friend to the growing boy—and their relationship, in spite of occasional clashes, was close.

The ground was leveling out now and the three men were able to ride abreast. Adam chose his words with care.

"I suppose your mind is made up? I'll allow the girl is no beauty, but . . ."

"She's a distempered freak!" Sir Roger volunteered with brutal frankness.

"She's a duke's daughter," said Adam with some asperity. "You're rising six and twenty, Theo—and, God knows, you've sown enough wild oats for ten men! It's high time you gave some thought to the business of settling down. In purely practical terms, you can't hope for a better match."

Irritation betrayed the Viscount into digging sharply with his heel; the hunter objected and began to caracole. There were a few moments of confusion while it was brought under control.

"I don't know why you ride that brute," Sir Roger observed unkindly, edging his own mount away. "Always said it had an unstable temperament."

"Better that than a sluggard!" retorted Theo with a pointed glance at his friend's docile bay. Then he turned his attention back to Adam. "You have but to add that I owe it to the family to marry and beget an heir and I shall begin to suspect that Gertrude wrote your speech for you," he said scathingly. "If that is your reason for coming up here, you have wasted your time. You know very well my stepmother cannot wait to claim a duke as kin! Her lack of breeding is never so blatantly obvious as when she is hatching and matching! She got de Beauville for Daisy by means of a downright scurvy trick, and when Letty comes out next year, only the Marriage Mart's most eligible property will do for her."

His voice hardened perceptibly. "Well, the girls are hers—she may maneuver them as she pleases, but *I'll* not dance to any tune of her piping, and so you may tell her!"

"I would as lief you told her yourself," said Adam firmly. "And while you are about it, you must make your intention—or lack of it—clear to Arren. He is hourly expecting you to seek his permission to pay your addresses."

"Then he'll wait in vain. Let my stepmother eat humble pie. It was her meddling stirred up the whole ghastly affair in the first place!"

Adam privately endorsed Theo's sentiments, yet felt obliged to say placatingly, "To be fair, Arren did approach her—or so Aunt Gertrude insists. Lord knows why he should wish to entrust his only daughter to you. . . ."

"Desperation?" suggested Sir Roger, sotto voce.

". . . but it seems there was some kind of tentative agreement when Eustacie was in the cradle. . . ."

"Not by me, there wasn't!"

"Stands to reason. It's as plain as the nose on your face!" Sir Roger said with damning finality. "The girl's not like to be offered for by any but a short-sighted imbecile! Can't really blame her father for suddenly calling to mind this affecting cradle-side pledge. It's a bag of moonshine, of course. Truth is, Theo—his ugly duckling is infatuated with you, and Papa intends to capitalize on it for all he's worth!"

"Well, he'll get short shrift from me," Theo said abruptly. "He can keep his inflated dowry—and his equally inflated daughter—and so I shall tell him if you force me into it. Not that they wouldn't have been damned lucky to get me, let me tell you, Ham! Cousin Adam may think me feckless, but the Gilmores can trace an unbroken line back to the Norman Conquest, and not many families can claim as much!"

Adam sighed and gave up the unequal struggle. There was no denying the dowry would have proved useful; not that Theo was exactly purse-pinched, but he had inherited his father's recklessness and partiality for games of chance. And Adam knew only too well how disastrously his uncle's vicarious ways had added to the burden of his office. Although never heard to utter open criticism, it had nevertheless come as a profound relief to him when the late Viscount had finally quit the world on a winning streak.

As for Lady Gilmore, there was no use hoping that she and Theo would ever come to terms. The late Viscount's second marriage had never been more than a makeshift; even the vast fortune she had brought with her had only made tolerable her plebian background and her ice-cold lack of charm.

Sir Roger grunted and put up a hand. "Damm-it—I must have drunk more than I thought! What time will it be, Theo?"

"Lord knows! It was well past midnight when we left Thorpe Grange."

"I'd hazard a guess it's nearer two o'clock," said Adam Carvray.

"Thought so." Sir Roger sounded perplexed. "Then will you tell me what the devil anyone would be doing kicking up such a plaguey cater-wauling at two in the morning?"

They could all hear it now. Light flickered through the trees; laughter was borne on the wind, and with it, the sound of a fiddle scraping away at some sort of gig.

The Viscount gave a shout. "Gypsies, by God! On my land!" He spurred his horse and went off at a gallop with the other two hard on his heels.

They rode in upon a scene of almost frenzied brilliance. The clearing was ringed by a straggling assortment of rough carts and tents; a fire hissed and crackled beneath a crudely fashioned spit, where a motionless bag of bones kept watch, one clawlike hand emerging from time to time to rotate the neatly skewered carcasses.

A number of torches were secured on poles and, teased by the gusty wind, the flames leaped with a riotous abandon to illuminate the stomping men and the women who whirled dizzily, their black skirts and colored petticoats whipping around bare brown legs.

The fiddler saw the trio first. His playing trailed

away on a thin, wailing discord and all movement ceased. The gypsies stood, proud and impassive, only the younger women betraying interest, staring with an open curiosity bordering on insolence.

No violence was offered to the intruders, yet a deep violence of spirit ran beneath the thin veneer of indifference. Adam sensed it and prayed that there would not be trouble. If only Theo would leave the talking to him.

But Theo was already leaning imperiously from the saddle, his restive hunter tight-curbed as its dilated nostrils picked up the pungent smell of smoke. A young, olive-skinned giant with the face of a Greek god stepped forward without hurry. He said something in a low, guttural tongue and ran a sure hand over the horse's neck. The animal shuddered once and was still.

"Who's in charge here?" Theo demanded.

The young gypsy lifted long, drooping eyelashes to give him back stare for stare.

"My father, Fergus Lovell, is our *sher-engro*," he said sullenly, indicating a large man shouldering his way to the front of his silent tribe.

"The young *Gorgios* are welcome in our camp." The geniality of the man's words was not reflected in the wary black eyes set too close in a dark cavern of a face. He was big. A faded blue jockey coat hung from massive shoulders and fawn breeches hugged thighs as solid as tree trunks.

"You come most opportunely." He indicated a young girl, more richly dressed than the rest, standing near the fire. "My daughter has this day married her cousin—a fine young Rom. He will make her a splendid husband and she will give him many sons . . ."

"You are trespassing," Theo cut in abruptly.

The gypsy's geniality did not diminish, but a certain hardness crept into his voice. "No so, brother. We have the owner's permission to stay here for the space of three days."

"I *am* the owner."

Theo swung from the saddle and the other two, anticipating trouble, did likewise, and came to stand at his shoulder. Torchlight threw up the arrogant contours of the Viscount's face, emphasized the dark, strongly springing hair drawn carelessly back into a queue.

"Damn me, if he don't look a bit of a gypsy himself!" murmured Sir Roger irrepressibly. One hand rested hopefully on the hilt of a light dress sword. "Will we need to fight our way out, think you?"

"I trust it won't come to that," Adam replied. "Young fool!"

The man Lovell's eyes had narrowed; he spread his hands and his tone grew more unctious. "Then you are the Lord Gilmore—and are thus doubly welcome. Your factor, Mr. Powell, it was who gave us leave to camp. I have his written permit, if you would see it?"

Theo frowned. Adam, fearful of his mood, laid a warning hand on his arm. Theo met Adam's eyes and anger left him as swiftly as it had come. He grinned.

"You are right, my dear. As always." He turned back to the gypsy. "Keep your permit. You are welcome to it," he said with careless grace.

"We would be honored if the *Gorgio* lord and his friends would stay awhile, to lend nobility to our festivities. Our hospitality is a poor thing, but we are at your feet."

The invitation, ingratiatingly offered, appealed to Theo's mood.

"Why not, indeed? Adam—Ham? How do you fancy a gypsy wedding feast to round off the evening?"

A decision having been reached, the atmosphere underwent a subtle change. The trio were not so much made welcome as accepted with a curious ambivalence. A chair was brought and covered with rugs fashioned from animal skins. More skins were laid on the ground, and these Sir Roger regarded with fastidious distaste.

"Must we?"

"Don't be so nice in your notions," said Theo, sprawling in the seat of honor.

They were plied with food and drink, the women offering the Viscount delicately roasted game—undoubtedly culled from his own covers—with a blandness that made Adam smile. The fine silver goblets brimming with pale amber liquid he viewed with suspicion and advised the others to drink sparingly; it would be home brewed—and potent!

Theo, his good humor largely restored, accused him of being a dull, unadventurous dog, but affection robbed the words of any sting.

If the gypsies invested the scene with its color and vitality, it was their guests who supplied the magnificence, and though Sir Roger's powdered head and rich silks were by far the finest, it was the Viscount who drew overt glances; not for the richness of his dress, or the unmistakable wink of diamonds in the lace at his throat—what attracted them was the singularly vivid, dark face, the cutaway nostrils, the bright restless eyes; a face that could surely claim kinship with the Romany.

On the far side of the camp raised voices began to attract attention; Fergus Lovell was arguing with a young girl, who looked slim and fragile beside his bulk. Both were angry. At last the man made an unmistakable gesture of finality and stalked away followed by a stream of words thrown in defiance.

"The girl will dance for you," Fergus Lovell stood before his guests and spoke abruptly. "She is very fine dancer." He jerked his head in the fiddler's direction.

This was a very different kind of music to anything that had gone before. It began with a slow, throbbing insistence. The girl, with obvious reluctance, began first to sway and then to encircle the fire in a rhythmic, stepping movement, slowly at first and then ever faster, her body undulating with extraordinary grace, her bare feet spinning, skimming the ground as the tempo increased.

Even the gray old fiddler seemed strangely affected, as though there was a magic running in his blood, flowing from his fingers into the bow and thence to caress the sobbing, singing strings of his beloved violin until they were one with the dancer's flying feet and swirling red petticoats.

"By God! That fiddler can play!" breathed Sir Roger.

"There is a legend, if you would hear it, brother."

He turned to see a woman of great antiquity, her face wrinkled as worn brown leather. She rocked ceaselessly back and forth, intoning the words in a high, sing-song voice.

"It is told how a beautiful gypsy girl once fell in love with a young *Gorgio* who would have none of her. In despair, the foolish *rackli* made a pact with the Devil, selling to him the souls of her family in exchange for his help. He made of her father, a sound box; of her four brothers, strings; and her mother became a bow . . . and out of their six souls was born the violin. The *rackli* learned to play this wondrous instrument and soon the handsome *Gorgio* was her slave."

Theo, at first no more than mildly interested, soon found his imagination stirred by the old woman's fable. He drained his goblet and leaned forward.

"But in her hour of triumph the Devil reappeared and carried them both to Hell. The violin lay forgotten until, one day a young Romany boy found it—and discovered its magic. Since that time, gypsies and violins have been inseparable."

The blood was beginning to thud in Theo's veins. Surely there was something unnatural about the girl's performance? As though she were being driven against her will? At times, she seemed suspended above the ground, her glorious black hair whipping about her face, her eyes brilliant, yet curiously blank of all expression, as if she were under the influence of some strong opiate.

At last the fiddler tired; on a final, crashing chord, the girl sank in an extraordinary gesture of obeisance at Theo's feet, her shoulders heaving with exhaustion. The cloud of hair, obscuring her face, trailed like ebony silk in the dust before him.

"Oh, Lord!" Adam breathed in dismay. "Theo's not the man to let such temptation pass! 'Ware trouble, Ham, my boy!"

But Sir Roger, like Theo, had been less than prudent with the contents of his goblet, which never seemed to grow any less. He beamed fatuously at Adam—and then at the prostrate girl.

"Can't say I'd altogether blame Gilmore," he said carefully. "Fascinating little piece!" His eyes brightened. "Dashed if I don't cut him out!"

He came uncertainly to his feet and lurched forward. Adam was obliged to restrain him, and in doing so lost any hope he might have had of changing the course of events.

Theo also stood up slowly, in the grip of a light-headed exhilaration. He lifted the gypsy bodily to her feet—and shock waves ran up his arms at the contact. Her head no more than tipped his shoulder; a deep-breasted, lissome armful! While he was still dwelling on her charms, she shook back her hair, angry contempt blazing in her eyes.

"Loose me, nobleman!" She spat the words at him, breathlessly, insultingly.

Theo looked taken aback; then he laughed. "When I have paid my tribute."

Before she could know what he was about, he had jerked her close and kissed her full on her parted mouth.

Retaliation was swift—and disconcertingly violent. Slight though she was, needle-sharp nails had already raked his cheek in stinging reprisal before both her hands were caught and held fast, inexorably forced down and clipped into the small of her back. Held thus close, she was powerless even to struggle. But with no such restraint on her tongue, she loosed a stream of invective.

"*Cabrón!*" She panted, drawing fresh breath. "*Hijo de mala leche!*"

"Little Spanish hellcat!" he retorted. Pinning her easily with one hand, he raised exploratory fingers to his face. "Dammit! You've drawn blood! You'll have to pay for that."

He found her mouth again and this time he lingered quite ruthlessly, reveling in the wild hammering of her heart; when at last he raised his head, she was gasping for air, her mouth trembling.

Theo held her savoring the moment; then, with a flick of the wrist sent her spinning to sprawl her length in the dust. She was up in an instant, crouched lightly on the balls of her feet; a knife gleamed in her hand and murder flared red in her eyes.

"Don't try it," he advised softly.

"Pilar!" Fergus Lovell came striding toward them with a face of thunder.

The girl uttered a sob of choked fury and swung on her heel, consigning them, individually and collectively, to the Devil.

"She shall apologize, lord," the chief said stiffly.

"Oh, let be, man. I provoked the wench beyond reason—she did no more than retaliate. I would have done as much in her place." Grudging admiration showed momentarily in Theo's eyes as he watched the bristling figure swing away out of sight. "We will take ourselves off—call it a night."

"You will not go until amends have been made. You are our guests. Furthermore, we are on your land and are thus *pazorrhus* to you. The Romany honors his debts."

Lovell stomped off in search of the girl. Theo flung himself down in the chair and reached for his goblet, which had been refilled yet again.

"Damned stupid fuss about nothing," he muttered.

"I'm glad you can think so," said Adam with commendable restraint. To say what he really felt would only provoke Theo in his present mood and perhaps cause further trouble. Sir Roger had lost interest in the proceedings and lay curled up fast asleep.

"*Aiya! Aiya!* The blood will always tell!" keened the old woman.

Theo stirred irritably in his chair. "And what might that cryptic observation mean, old crone?"

The gypsy sucked at a battered pipe, her rheumy eyes fixed on remote horizons. "It is not the Romany way, to loose anger at a guest, brother . . . but the poor *chavi* is not to blame. She was never accepted here."

"Because she is Spanish?" Adam asked, surprised.

The woman rocked steadily. "What is that to us?. Our people roam the earth, brother."

"Then why?" demanded Theo.

"I will tell you. Her mother stumbled into our camp one night . . . already the mark of the grave was on her. We could make little of her story, save that she had been for many years an outcast among her own . . . dishonored by an English gentile—a fine *raior*, even as yourself—who had abandoned her in her need.

"At last, with a sickness upon her, she crossed the sea in search of him, bringing with her the child of her disgrace. But time had run out for her. Pilar was then some twelve years . . . a strange, wild creature. Fergus elected to keep her, but it was a decision not welcomed by some, who thought her *mokardi*—unclean."

"So the girl is only part gypsy?" Theo spoke half to himself, but the old crone's sharp ears picked up the words. Her head moved in weary negation.

"That is a hard thing to be, brother, perhaps the hardest of all, for both sides withhold true kinship. *Aiya!* It is a long, lonely road the poor one must travel, and who is to know what she may hope for at the end of it. . . ." The voice faded to a soft keening; she was away in her own world again.

The girl was coming back. She walked stiffly, as though each step pained her. In the background the massive figure of Fergus Lovell stood, wide-legged and truculent, buckling on his crude leather belt. Many pairs of eyes watched her come, and there was sly laughter among the women.

She stopped before Theo, stared fixedly at a spot beyond his left ear, choked on the beginning of an apology, stumbled, and in desperation began again.

Theo stood up—and the ground swayed crazily under his feet. He put his hands on the girl's shoulders to steady himself, and noticed that she flinched. A small knot of anger moved inside him.

"Beat you, did he? A pity . . . I would not have had you so used. 'Tis a poor reward for such a brave show of spirit." His eyes were compellingly, mockingly intent, but though she stiffened under his hands, she would not look at him. Her lack of response goaded him to see if he could provoke her further. "Yet, I confess, you disappoint me strangely. I had not thought you so easy to subdue."

That brought her glance around, sparked a leaping flame of rebelliousness. It burned for an instant and died.

"Think what you will," she said tonelessly.

"You don't like me overmuch, do you?"

"It is not necessary that I like you. Take my apology, lord, and let me be."

"And if I decline?" Some devil was prompting Theo to prolong the moment. The girl's closeness tantalized him. In the light from the torches her skin glowed with the golden warmth of ripe apricots in the sun, each finely molded cheekbone dusted with a blush of color. He remembered how softly that skin had lain against his own. And that full, beguiling mouth set now in sullen lines—he knew it for a traitor!

"Please, lord!" The mouth trembled.

Behind him, Adam said quietly, "Let her go, Theo."

Theo's brow lifted. "There speaks the voice of wisdom, child. But my cousin knows, none better, what a creature of perversity I am. And 'twas a grudging enough apology you offered me, in all truth! I am not sure that I should let you off so lightly."

He had roused her to anger at last. "Odious one!" she cried, and then, biting her lip, "Ah, no! I must not . . . I will not!"

Panic flickered for a moment in the eyes locked furiously with his own. It intrigued him. Such wild, dark eyes. He wished there were light enough to determine their color.

"You are wise to hold your tongue, little firebrand," he murmured. "To quarrel with me now would doubtless earn you a further beating, which would please neither of us."

She jerked her head away scornfully, "I fear nothing that Fergus Lovell can do to me."

"There's a fine, bold statement! And well timed, for he is coming across." Theo felt a distinct tremor beneath his hands and was further intrigued. His hands tightened. "Yet you *are* afraid, my bird. I wonder why?"

The chief's voice boomed. "So, my Lord Gilmore. Has this wicked, ungrateful *rackli* abased herself before you?"

In the silence that followed there were all man-

ner of undercurrents; eyes turned to the group
where Adam had now risen, his anger barely contained. But Theo was hardly aware of him, or of
anyone else. His attention was wholly centered
upon the young gypsy, who had grown suddenly
tense, as though bracing herself for his denunciation.

"The girl has done everything one might reasonably expect of her," he said curtly and felt a long,
slow shudder run through her. "She is exonerated
of all blame. I ask only that she may remain here
with us for the present."

"You hear, Pilar?" boomed Fergus pompously.
"Know, then, that you are more fortunate than you
deserve. Stay, as you are bid, and let me hear no
more of rebellion."

With the man's going the tensions eased. Adam
sighed his relief. Theo was still holding the young
gypsy, as though loath to release her. She was very
quiescent. He looked down and surprised in her
eyes an unnatural brilliance; she blinked impatiently and a tear, jewel bright, ran in a glittering
rivulet down her cheek. He took a fine lace handkerchief from his pocket and wiped it away, well
aware of her suspicion.

"Well, Pilar?" he queried softly. "Beautiful,
proud Pilar. A fine, bewitching name—well suited
to its owner, wouldn't you say, Adam?"

She sprang away from him as though at bay—as
though she would turn and run but for the still-
hovering figure of the chief. The suddenness of her
move caused Theo to sway back unsteadily on his
heels.

"Deuce take it! Now what have I said?"

She eyed him warily. "It is what you have not

said. The words fall like honey from your lips, lord, with practiced ease, as befits your kind. But I am not such a fool, let me tell you, that I should be so easily seduced."

"Seduced!" Theo spluttered. "Because I save you from that old goat's wrath and toss you a compliment or so? You've a damned queer notion of seduction!"

Not so, lord," she came back at him with surprising confidence. "For now you will expect me to say *muchas gracias* and repay you for your kindness. Is this not so?"

"I might just do that, baggage! You'd be well served! Egad, there's no pleasing you, it seems!"

"My dear young lady," Adam broke in with a reassuring smile. "You wrong my cousin in this instance. I believe he means you no harm, though his manner may suggest otherwise." He made the bewildered girl an elegant leg. "Permit me to introduce myself—Adam Carvray at your service."

Theo grunted his admiration. "Marvelous, ain't it? He goes on like that all the time, you know. Devilish proper, is Cousin Adam."

Pilar stared from him to the polite one, who treated her as a queen—and from him her glance went to the third man, who lay like a painted doll among the fur skins, his mouth open, snoring loudly. Her expression said plainly that they were mad, the lot of them!

Theo indicated his recumbant friend. "The sleeping exquisite is Sir Roger Hammell. I fear he has partaken too well of your friends' hospitality. Will you sit?"

She eyed the proffered chair uneasily and then shook her head and squatted nearby on the rug.

"As you will." Theo shrugged and flung himself

down in the chair, where he sat regarding her with a brooding intentness while Adam leaned against the side of one of the carts.

"So little *malvada*?" Her head came up in surprise. "Yes, I know a little of your native tongue—enough to appreciate your opinion of me a little while back!" Thick lashes came down swiftly to veil her eyes. "Quite so," he said dryly. "Now, suppose you tell me what dire threat that old goat holds over you that makes you so afraid?"

Her silent profile was sullenly aloof, almost to the point of arrogance. Theo's voice sharpened.

"Come—you don't lack courage. You have already proved as much. Yet something just now reduced you to a shaking terror. I would know what that thing is."

"You would not understand," she muttered.

"Try me."

Adam said mildly, "If the child doesn't wish to honor you with her confidence . . ."

"Nonsense! Why should she balk at the telling?"

Pilar gave in with an impatient gesture. "There is little enough to tell. I am in trouble . . . oh, many times since I came to these people! I am *ingrata* because I do not submit without question to their laws. It has earned me many beatings . . . of late, Fergus has protested how it grieves him that he must still take his belt to me!" There was scorn in her voice. "But I have seen his eyes."

"Enjoys it, does he?"

"More than a man should, lord—and when the man has a wife, that is unwise. She hates me, as do many of the women, because of what I am. . . ." Here she faltered.

Theo said impatiently, "Yes, yes, we have heard something of your history. Go on."

"Finding that he could not beat an apology out of me, Fergus turned instead to threats. I would do as he said, or . . ." Here again she stopped, and then flung her head back as though challenging them to make light of it. ". . . or I would be delivered up to his wife and her intimates for chastisement."

Adam exclaimed, and Theo leaned forward in sudden interest. "A pack of vengeful women! Dear God! I have heard tales. . . ."

"Whatever you have heard, lord, you may believe ten times worse—a hundred times, even! I have endured it once only, and vowed that never again would I submit to such humiliation." The words were uttered with a choked intensity that disturbed even Theo.

Before more could be said, however, there was a stirring and the gypsies began to form up into a wide circle.

"Hello! What now?" said Adam.

"They are to have the ceremonies," Pilar explained. "Each tribe has its betrothal ceremonies. They set a seal upon the marriage vows."

The *sher-engro* had taken from one of the carts a cumbersome leather bag with a heavy curved bar across the top. He placed it on the ground and removed from it all the tools of his tinker's trade, keeping only the blunt-nosed vice. This he propped upright in the bag, and taking a pair of wax candles, secured them in its jaws and lit them.

With great solemnity the young couple were brought before their chief—the girl shy and tremulous, her eyes modestly lowered—the man with a confident swagger. They were placed back to back beside the candles.

With impressive authority the chief intoned the

ritual in his own tongue; at a given signal the couple walked away from one another to come face to face on the other side of the candles, then turned and retraced their steps.

"He is telling them to turn and hurry back to greet the unborn of their tribe," Pilar translated in a whisper.

Now the couple were turned to face the candles. On a stern command, the girl gathered her bright skirts close, looked apprehensively at the dancing flames, and leaped, light as a gazelle, the ribbons of her lace headdress streaming out behind her. The candle flames dipped and then steadied. A sigh went through the watchers and, as the girl whirled around with a little skirl of joy, the man jumped high and confidently to meet her.

The *sher-engro*'s figure loomed portentously as he bent to snuff the candles between his fingers with a final solemn incantation.

"So life goes—without a flicker." Pilar's face was shuttered, her voice filled suddenly with a somber fatalism.

Adam said bracingly, "Very impressive."

She roused with an effort. "Now the couple lead the wedding dance."

Amid the growing babel of sound the fiddler struck an opening chord. "You see? It only begins, now. There will be more noise—more feasting and much more drinking—it will go on until they drop."

Theo came to his feet unsteadily. "Well then." He extended a peremptory hand. "Let us show your barbarian of a chief how well you have learned your lesson. I have a fancy to participate in this extraordinary celebration."

While she still hung back, he swooped, his hands encompassing her waist, and swung her to her feet.

Against her will, his eyes dominated hers, and in a moment they were lost in the swirl of bodies.

Much later Adam saw them, breathless and laughing, and was disturbed to note that Theo still held the girl possessively in the curve of his arm. He watched, in dismay, as Theo reached for a goblet and, still laughing, put it first to her lips and then his own.

Theo, in fact, was in the grip of a wonderfully liberating sensation. He tipped Pilar's face up to see it better. "You should laugh more often, *hija*," he said deeply. "It makes liquid fire of your eyes!"

His arm tightened urgently and she began to struggle. "No, no, lord! Let me go! Oh, please, do not make trouble for me! You know what will happen!"

"Then don't fight me."

"I must!" He could feel her trembling. "Do you suppose I do not know what it is you want of me? Because I am gypsy, you think me loose. But you are wrong! A Romany woman guards her honor above all."

"But you are only half Romany," he murmured persuasively.

"*Insensato!*" She pulled away in anger. "My mother was betrayed! Do you think I am so stupid that I would follow the same path? Her noble *Gorgio* lord even tricked her with talk of marriage. He promised to bring her to England, but he went away and she never saw him again. It was clear that he thought better of his foolishness. Can you not imagine how his family would receive such a bride?"

Theo's eyes were blazing with the dawning of some inner excitement. "Oh, I can, indeed!. Come." He seized her hand and dragged her, protesting, back to where Adam had made himself comfortable in the chair. "Coz—your felicitations. I have decided to heed your good advice and get married!"

2

"No!" cried Pilar, struggling to free herself.

Adam looked from one to the other and slowly got to his feet. "If this is a joke, Theo, I can only say I consider it in deplorable taste!"

"Devil a bit!" retorted Theo. " 'Tis a jest of the first order—a capital idea! Can you not imagine my fond stepmamma's face when I walk in with my gypsy bride on my arm?"

"I can," said Adam grimly. "I know also what will be the reaction of others. Sometimes, Theo, you convince me that you are hell-bent on destroying yourself."

"Humbug, coz! You have no vision. Think how diverting it will be to make a lady of this young savage!"

"No!" Unable to make her presence felt any other way, Pilar resorted to beating her free fist against the *Gorgio*'s chest. It was immediately caught and held. "Release me! I am not savage! I have told you . . . I will have no part of this madness!"

"Be silent." Theo held her away a little, looking her over critically, but with growing enthusiasm. "Damn me, if we couldn't do it, y'know! See how she carries her head? The chit was born to be a Viscountess!"

"Let her go, Theo." Adam spoke sharply. "This tomfoolery has gone far enough. Wake Ham and come home with me now—at once. It has been a long night and you are very much the worse for wear. You'll thank me in the morning."

Even as the words were out, he knew he was speaking to the air. What had begun as a heady inspiration born of the wine and the romantic extravagance of this strange world they had stumbled into, had now become an obsession. What the outcome would be, he scarcely dared to contemplate! Theo's voice was bordering on petulance.

"You're being 'dog in the manger,' Cousin Adam! I tell you—I'd as lief wed my little gypsy as Arren's pudding-faced brat any day of the week. And she does have some good, noble blood flowing in her veins, even if we ain't certain whose it is!"

"Precisely!"

Theo shot him a frowning look, then his brows lifted in amusement. "Oh, no, my dear—not that! Not my reprehensible parent! His vices were legion, I'll grant you, but his fancy never ran to petticoats, that I ever heard!"

"*Basta!* Enough!" Realizing the futility of struggling, Pilar bent in desperation and sank her teeth into the rich lace at Theo's wrist. He swore and slackened his hold. At once she sprang back, a hand to her throat, her eyes sheening with angry tears. "I will endure no more! Do you think I have no feelings?" She was choking on the words. "Listen to me, both of you . . . I am *me* . . . do you hear? *Me*, not some mindless one to be used for your ends! You shall not trick me, as my poor mother was tricked! No! *Absolutemente!* No!"

She turned and fled into the darkness beyond the camp. Theo swore again and started after her.

"Leave her, lord. She will be punished."

Lovell stood in his path; at his side, a woman, thin-lipped, hard-eyed, implacable enough to chill the blood, oily hair scraped back tight from a sallow face.

The Viscount looked them over with arrogant contempt. "Is that all you can think about? I don't want her punished, curse you. I want to marry her!"

"Theo—for pity's sake!"

"And since she is in your charge," he swept on, regardless of Adam's plea, "I believe I must apply to you for her hand."

The two gypsies were stunned into silence by this totally unexpected turn of events. The woman recovered first. She was at once coldly businesslike.

"We would not stand in the girl's light, lord," she said smoothly. "But she is a good worker—young and strong—and we are loath to part with her. You understand me, lord?"

Theo's lip curled. The scheming, lying she-devil! Aloud he said curtly, "I understand. You want money. How much?"

She appeared to give the matter thought, glanced at her husband, and said obliquely, "That is a fine horse you ride, lord."

Impatient to leave and very much aware of Adam's protests, he snapped, "I'll not part with Zenda, but if that is your price, I have a young stallion in my stable every bit as good. It will be delivered to you at first light . . . when you will leave my land." As she hesitated, he added brusquely, "I don't bargain. Those are my terms."

Lovell was like a man cornered. The gypsy in him knew well what an acquisition such a fine young horse would be, yet he still lusted after the girl.

"What will Jem say? You know he's hot for her." His show of bluster fooled no one. "Our son, lord. He is at the age when a man hankers after a maid. He regards Pilar as his woman." The protest had a hollow ring, even in his own ears.

"No!" His wife swept him a contemptuous look. She was very positive—very final. "There is no question of a betrothal. The girl is yours, lord. But you must take her now—tonight—and she may never return."

Theo stared for a moment, swaying slightly with the effort of concentrating, then nodded curtly. "Agreed," he said, and plunged off in the direction Pilar had taken.

He crashed through the undergrowth with little attempt at stealth, and found her at length in a small clearing deep in the woods. She made as though to run, and then shrugged and stood passively.

"Little fool," he said roughly. "You might have fallen foul of my keepers!"

Again she shrugged. "It matters little to me."

He turned her face up to the moon's light; shimmering with the traces of spent tears, its delicate molding seemed to be wrought from pure silver. But shadows gave her full lower lip a fierce, truculent pout and her eyes were unyielding. His hands tightened on her shoulders and his voice thickened.

"I have your chief's consent."

The thick lashes veiled her expression. "You do not have mine."

"Would you prefer to stay and face the wrath of that charming vixen, his wife?" There was no reaction beyond a slight tremor. "Perhaps you hope to wed her son? Well, forget it—she will never permit it."

Still no answer. Impatience sharpened his voice. He shook her. "Dammit, girl! I am offering you a position most young ladies of high rank would give much to attain! There is, at this moment, a duke's daughter I could have for the asking."

"Then take her, lord," she said simply. "For you would be a fool to put me in her place."

An unwilling laugh broke from him. "Egad! You haven't seen her! Listen to me." The thing was fast becoming a matter of pride; the ingrate must be made to understand what she would be missing. "You will have fine dresses—as many as you please—beautiful houses, servants to do your bidding. You will be 'my Lady Gilmore,' received by the highest in the land."

She moved under his hands. "Do you suppose my mother was also told such tales?"

"My God, you are stubborn!" He thrust her away in a sudden violent uprush of revulsion. "I'm obviously wasting my time. Forget the whole idea. Stay here, little fool, to be schooled by that black-hearted, vindictive shrew—and may God have mercy on you, for most assuredly she will have none!"

He strode unsteadily between the trees, a red mist of fury before his eyes. In a moment there was a rush of feet; urgent fingers tugged at his arm.

"Lord . . . wait!" Tears were making her voice husky. "I am confused . . . *en nombre de Dios!* It makes no sense! Why would you marry a gypsy . . . a stranger, not even of your kind? It must be the wine speaking in your blood . . . if you would only wait . . ."

"No. It must be now, tonight." He didn't slacken

pace and she had to run, stumbling, through the undergrowth to keep up with him.

"And if you change your mind with the morning?" He did halt then, staring down at her with brows lowered. "Can you not see how it will be?" she pleaded. "I shall be quite without support, for these people will never take me back."

"You have my word. The word of a Gilmore should suffice."

She stared back, mutinously silent. Deep in the wood, a nightingale poured out its song of love, unnoticed.

"Egad!" he said softly. "You don't balk at insults, do you?"

"I am sorry," she said, sounding anything but repentant. "But I do not know how honorable are the Gilmores, lord. You cannot blame me if I judge your nobility by the only standards I know."

Theo grunted. "Very well, little malcontent. It seems we must knock up the preacher."

Pilar peered up at him as though he were indeed mad. "At this hour? Will he consent to perform such a ceremony?"

"He will if he knows what's good for him!" drawled the Viscount derisively. "And I doubt the Reverend Dunwoody will care to jeopardize his so comfortable living over so trivial a matter."

She was not noticeably reassured. "You think marriage trivial? Or only this particular marriage? Perhaps I should not trust this padre, either. My mother. . . ."

"Forget your mother!" Theo exploded irritably. "Untrusting little baggage! Look, you shall have Cousin Adam for witness. Will that satisfy you? Even you could not suspect Adam of treachery!"

Adam, however, when told of their intention,

thought it no trivial matter. He declared bluntly that he would have no part of it.

"Oh, but you must, senor!" Pilar pleaded. "Who is to safeguard my honor if you do not go with us?"

"She ain't disposed to take the word of a Gilmore," said the Viscount mockingly, taking out his snuff box and helping himself to a liberal pinch. "So you'll have to swallow your scruples for once, my dear. Besides, you will lend a much needed air of respectability to the proceedings. Dunwoody's ruffled feathers might need smoothing."

"I beg you to reconsider, both of you!" Adam had the look of a man staring disaster in the face, without the means to turn it aside. "Theo, this is madness! And madness that you will bitterly regret."

"Well, if I do, I'll not come crying to you, my cousin." Theo turned abruptly to Pilar. "Have you any gewgaws to pack? We've wasted enough time." Sir Roger still lay snoring; Theo stirred him with a toe. "Wake up, Ham. You are invited to a wedding."

A snore, strangled in mid-flight, hovered and subsided into a gentle belch. Sir Roger opened bloodshot eyes. "Wassat? Did someone say wedding?"

Adam bent down to hoist him to his feet. "Ham—I told you not ten minutes since—pull yourself together, man! Talk to Theo, for God's sake! Perhaps you can make him see sense!" He looked into the painfully narrowed eyes and groaned. "Never mind. You are in worse case than he is."

The word *wedding*, however, had impinged itself stubbornly upon Ham's addled senses. "Wedding, you said. Whose wedding?"

"Theo's. He's as drunk as beddam—and bent on marrying that girl!"

"Theo!" Sir Roger staggered upright and peered into the Viscount's lean, dark face. "Don't do it, m'boy!" he urged. "That Friday-faced brat of Arren's may be hot for you, now, but take my word for't, she'll be frigid just like her ma . . . always do take after their mothers . . . noticed it most particularly . . ."

"Ham," Adam explained with diminishing patience, "we are not speaking of Lady Eustacie. Theo is set on marrying the gypsy girl—now—in the middle of the night."

"Gypsy girl?" There was a moment of frowning concentration and then Ham's face cleared. "Oh, yes—of course! That's a'right, then. Now there *is* an armful worth the having! Sensible fellow, Theo . . . always said so. . . ." He smiled beatifically and Adam gave up.

Word of Pilar's leaving had spread fast. The gypsies stood in stony silence as she threaded her way between them, head high, looking neither to right nor left. Her possessions, the accumulation of seventeen years, made an insignificant bundle, tied in a shawl and slung across her shoulder, and with every graceful stride, her hips swung defiantly.

No voice wished her well—or ill. No hand was offered. Never popular, she was now doing the unforgivable; she was marrying a gentile. From this night she would never be spoken of again.

The young gypsy who had spoken on their arrival, brought the horses forward and the three men mounted. As Pilar approached, he stepped forward to bar her path, his eyes smoldering in a sullen face.

"You would go with this *Gorgio*? In spite of what is between us?"

"There is nothing between us, Jem." A quick spasm crossed her face and was gone. "There never could be. You must know that. It is better for me to go."

"Go then. And take my curses with you!" he said deeply, and strode away, pushing his way through the wall of silent watchers. Pilar stared at his retreating back with a look of complete desolation.

The Viscount had witnessed the exchange. The words were strange to him, but the message was clear enough. He called Pilar's name, and she turned quickly, almost blindly. He leaned down and took her bundle to hook it onto his saddle; then he reached a hand to her and in a lithe movement she lifted a bare foot to his boot and was swung up to sit before him. The arm which came to encircle her waist was as much a declaration of possession as the look which accompanied the gesture.

She shivered a little. And then her glance fell on Fergus Lovell; he had the tortured look of a man about to lose that which he had never quite had the nerve to possess; it pointed, quite sharply, the difference between the two men, but brought her little comfort. Her glance shifted to Lovell's wife, who was no longer bothering to conceal her feelings.

And then they were moving; with a signal to his companions, the Viscount wheeled his horse. Before they were clear of the camp, the fiddle was skirling and the celebrations were in full cry again as though there had been no interruption.

They were already forgotten.

3

Mr. Dunwoody, snug in the depths of a luxurious featherbed, was dreaming of Dr. Arbuthnot's new maid, Nancy—a nubile creature with red hair and a figure which even a shapeless dress could not disguise. The Reverend preached mortification of the flesh with great fervor from his pulpit, yet he was a man for all that, and a man cannot be held answerable for his dreams.

He missed the ring of horses' hooves as they clattered down the silent village street; was reluctant to abandon the teasing promise in a pair of laughing blue eyes, even when the hammering on the door grew insistent. Only when a stone rapped sharply on his window did he sit up with a jerk, muttering an expletive that would have astounded his parishioners.

By the time he thrust his head angrily through the open window, several other windows in the street were going up, and there were testy demands to know what the —— was going on.

Mr. Dunwoody's querulous complaints died as the figure of his patron detached itself from the knot of horses on the silvered cobbles below.

"By heaven! You're hard to rouse! Stir yourself, man! I've work for you."

Fleeting recollections of the fading dream caused

guilty color to surge into Mr. Dunwoody's podgy face and he was thankful for the darkness. He hurried into his clothes and went down to admit his callers.

Soon he was leading the way, by bobbing lantern light, into the darkened church, his more than ample flesh quaking under the enormity of what was being demanded of him.

From the chancel steps he turned to peer down at his headstrong patron. "My lord, this is most irregular!" he wailed. "Not even a special license! For aught I know, this young person may be acting under duress . . . or in ignorance, mayhap. I need time . . . Oh, sir! I do urge you most earnestly to reconsider!"

The ill-lit, echoing cavern took his words, bounced them off the bleak stone walls, and tossed them mockingly back at him.

Sir Roger, who had taken little part in the proceedings up to now, leaned forward and squinted up into the clergyman's face. "Dammit, Theo! I wouldn't let this sour-faced, pontificating bag o' wind marry me! That face'd turn the cream . . . cast a blight on the nuptials!"

"He can look as sour as he pleases, an' he performs the ceremony," Theo said shortly.

Mr. Dunwoody was a timid man; a man palpably unequal to the prospect of doing battle with his patron, and showing clear evidence that he was beginning to crack under the strain. But the situation was such as to rouse in him the strongest moral scruples. The girl was one of that traveling band of gypsies if he wasn't mistaken! Such marriages were not unheard of when strong passions held sway, but this girl appeared almost indifferent, and the only evidence of passion he could discern in his lordship arose from ill-temper and an impatience to get the whole thing over and done with.

He cleared his throat nervously. "My lord, I am persuaded that I should stand firm in my refusal to proceed."

There was an uncomfortable moment of silence, and then: "Do that, my friend," warned the Viscount in his soft, silky voice, "and I take the wench to wife without benefit of clergy."

"No!" Pilar cried.

"My lord—I protest!"

"Protest all you like," his lordship continued, ignoring the girl's cry and dropping the words with gentle insistence into the dank, cheerless air. "But, refuse me—and I promise you will be out of this living so fast, you'll feel the draught! *And* I shall make it my business to see you don't secure another in a hurry."

This hit Mr. Dunwoody where it hurt. He was more than content with this small country living, which made few demands upon him. His lower lip began to quiver.

"Theo! Guard your tongue, for pity's sake," pleaded Adam Carvray. "You aren't helping matters, you know."

"Don't you believe it, coz. This old scoundrel has been the comfortable recipient of my family's benevolence for a great many years. In all that time, no one has interfered with him. The time has come for him to show a little appreciation."

Adam Carvray shrugged, acknowledging the futility of further protestation. "Mr. Dunwoody," he said, not unkindly, "His lordship is unshakably set on this marriage. So, much as I deplore its hasty conception, I believe that in everyone's best interests, not least the young lady's, I must advise you to proceed."

Mr. Dunwoody, relieved to have the guidance of a man of sense, capitulated without further demur, and the ceremony was allowed to proceed, but with so much bickering as to make it, in his eyes, a mockery. By far the hottest argument arose over the discovery that there was no ring; it culminated in the Viscount's pulling off his own signet ring with a gesture of impatience.

"Here. This will suffice," he snapped, and pushed it clumsily over the knuckle of Pilar's slim, brown finger, where the heavy, embossed head at once slipped around so that she was obliged to close her fist over it.

Sir Roger, by this time in rollicking good humor, pronounced the whole a damned dull affair—more of a wake than a wedding—and attempted to enliven the proceedings with a lusty and blatantly sacrilegious rendition of: "Teach me to live that I may dread/the grave as little as my bed," culled from dim recollections of his childhood and a youth misspent at Harrow.

The formalities completed, the young gypsy came to life, demanding the necessary document proving her marriage beyond all doubt.

The sorely tried clergyman glanced nervously at Lord Gilmore. "Oh, give it her, for goodness sake, man! I've better things to do with what's left of the night than spend it in this draughty mausoleum!"

The girl took the paper, eyed it suspiciously, and thrust it at Mr. Carvray. "I will trust you to tell me," she said defiantly. "Is it in order, please?"

He assured her with gravity that it was, and she tucked it carefully away in her bodice.

Bumping along again, with the pommel of Lord

Gilmore's saddle prodding her constantly in the back, Pilar struggled with a growing sense of unreality. She pressed a fiercely protective hand against her bodice, where the precious piece of paper reposed, not caring that its sharp edge cut into her. It lay like a weapon—like her knife, which she had used to good effect many times! This weapon, too, she would use to fight for her rightful place—if fight she must—as her gentle mother had never been able to do.

This lord who was now her husband should not so easily be rid of her! She, Pilar, would learn and learn quickly. It would not be so difficult; she had seen fine ladies aplenty; they came to the traveling fairs in their silks and laces, stepping daintily from elegant carriages and feigning horror at the sight of the poor, unkempt gypsies. Well—they did not know what came to them, for a poor gypsy would outshine them all! Had not old Ursula read her future, and prophesied greatness? Pilar's stomach felt squeezed tight as she remembered suddenly how the old woman had fallen silent and looked at her strangely, and when pressed, had muttered about conflict . . . and fire . . . and brother set against brother. She shrugged her uneasiness away; she had not heeded the words then—foolish to let them bother her now.

The man they called Sir Roger had been singing since they left the church, and by the time they stopped before a house, etched square and unwelcoming against the night sky, Lord Gilmore had lifted his own deeper voice in somewhat doubtful harmony.

He slithered from the saddle and reached uncertain hands to Pilar's waist, swung her down, and took a firmer grip.

"Don't drop the wench!" Sir Roger advised earnestly. "Could be dashed unlucky!"

"Let me down, lord!" Pilar protested.

His arms tightened. "Later. Must do the thing in prime style!"

Mr. Carvray, after one disgusted look, went up the steps without speaking and in a moment light was spilling down on them from a branch of candles held high by a startled manservant, who was obliged to step back hurriedly as Pilar, still protesting, was carried at a staggering run across the threshold into a gloomy hall where more candles were being hastily lit.

An older man in blue livery and wearing a neat tie wig appeared from the darkness and began giving orders in a calm, unhurried manner. Lord Gilmore hailed him good-humoredly.

"Ah—Fredericks! Her la'ship's room? All prepared, is it?"

My lord's valet, having been made cognizant of the situation, was able to parry the query with an admirable degree of composure, averting his eyes discreetly as he did so from the young person still supported uncertainly in his lordship's arms, her black hair tumbled in profusion against his coat and displaying more leg than could be considered seemly.

"A moment, only, my lord," he said primly. "Bridie is this minute engaged in warming the covers and lighting a fire, the room being somewhat chilly."

"You're a good fellow, Fredericks! Did I ever tell you so? You must wish me happy, you know . . . tied the knot this very night, all right and tight. Leg shackled at last . . . should settle my fond stepmamma, don't you think? Been angling to bring it about this twelvemonth or more."

Fredericks looked straight at Pilar and the accusation and distress that flickered momentarily in his eyes filled her with a burning resentment. As though the blame were hers!

The look was gone and Fredericks said quietly, "Just as you say, my lord. If you would come upstairs, now—I believe all should be ready for you."

She was carried past curious servants, up the stairs, and along corridors, feeling more stifled, more a prisoner with every passing moment. It was not possible to stay in this house full of dark shadows and hostile faces! A door opened and closed with a thud of finality and she was tossed unceremoniously onto a bed like a huge box, hung with suffocating curtains and topped with a domed lid carved out of solid, blackened oak.

The Viscount stood over her, swaying slightly, a queer, mocking light in his eyes.

"So, my dear wife. We are home at last!"

All her panic welled to the surface. She scrambled to her knees. "No, wait. Oh, please! I cannot . . . you must not . . ."

"Must not?" A quick frown turned to soft laughter at the sight of her crouched on the bed in wild disarray, as though poised for flight. To Pilar, the laugh seemed cruel. "Very well, my heart's jewel!" he drawled. "I'll not rush you. The rest of the night is ours, after all. You may have a little time to subdue your maidenly terrors and make yourself ready for me." He gestured expansively toward the door of an adjoining room. "A few minutes, mind . . . no more, and then I return."

The door clicked shut behind him, but Pilar made no move until a sound made her spin around.

There was a girl—a servant. She must have been there all the time, listening, and now stood eyeing her with open contempt as the hot shame flooded her face.

"Why do you stand there, fool?" Pilar demanded.

Without a word the girl walked to a cupboard and returned to spread out on the bed a delicate ivory silk nightgown and matching wrap edged with fur. Her glance lifted to make obvious comparisons with the dress Pilar wore.

"I'm to help *your ladyship* undress." There was resentment as well as insolence in the flat statement; enough to make Pilar round on her in a fury, driving her from the room.

Left alone, she eyed the gown with mounting apprehension; touched the pale gossamer folds with tentative fingers, shocked to the core by its indecency. Only a very bad sort of woman would flaunt herself in such a garment! I will not wear it, she vowed passionately. If the *Gorgio* lord is angered . . . at this point her cheeks began to burn again. Soon he would come. She clasped one of the carved bedposts for comfort, pressing her face against its rough surface. And there she stayed, while a little French clock on the mantleshelf chimed the passing of time and her heart's pounding eased to a steady, drumming beat. But, though it leaped afresh with every sound from the next room, he did not come.

The fire died; the candles burned lower and began to gutter. The pool of light around the bed was growing smaller. A satyr's head leered down from the bedpost—came nearer; the whole dome was coming nearer! Soon she would be unable to breathe!

Without knowing how she moved, she was on her feet and running to the door, her only thought to get away into the night. The man, Fredericks, was coming soft-footed down the passage. She stood with her back to the door. He hesitated and came toward her.

Pilar caught her breath on a sob. "Help me!" Had she said the words? He came nearer, looking puzzled.

"There was something you wanted, my lady?"

The politely voiced query made her want to laugh, but if once she began, it would be difficult to stop. She stared at him, wild-eyed, and saw in his eyes something akin to pity. Did he, then, know how she felt?

Fredericks, misinterpreting her panic, said not unkindly, "Lord Gilmore has . . . ahem . . . fallen asleep, ma'am. I doubt he will stir before the morning."

Was it for reassurance he spoke, or to invite her escape? Now that it offered itself, escape became the last thing she wanted. She drew herself up haughtily. "*Gracias*," she said, and went back into the room.

Unable to face the monstrous bed, she dragged the quilt over to the window, and there at last she slept.

A wood pigeon was croo-crooing close by. Pilar stirred, feeling the morning air cool on her face. She floundered through the receding mists of sleep with a curious lethargy, reluctant to admit reality. But the pigeon was most insistent, and so she opened her eyes—and remembered. Above her head, heavy brocade curtains moved fitfully in a capricious breeze. She sat up and flung them back, and sunshine flooded in, bringing with it all the blessedly familiar sounds and smells of morning.

Immediately below the window a magnolia tree spread elegant branches. Beyond, sprawled an ill-kempt garden, and in the blue-gray distance the bordering Westmorland fells rose out of a milky haze, still faintly etched with the pink of sunrise.

By day the room looked less frightening; in fact it was quite pretty—a room made for a lady, with lots of looking glasses on the walls. The cupboards proved to be full of beautiful dresses, and underfoot a thick carpet warmed her toes . . . discoveries both pleasant and surprising.

Only the bed was still awesome, with its massive canopy and thick carved posts with their evil, leering heads and shaggy, clawed feet. Even so, it had been foolish to be so afraid.

There was no sound from the room beyond. Was the *Gorgio* lord still sleeping? He has a poor head for our gypsy wine, she decided scornfully, and felt a quite irrational anger at his slighting of her. On the heels of her anger came the fear that he might seek to deny the events of the previous night.

Pilar drew the paper from her bodice and unfolded it, wishing that she could read the words. How insignificant a document it looked and yet it had changed her life. It must be hidden lest he try to take it from her. Her bundle lay incongruously upon a richly padded chair, and thrusting her hand inside, Pilar withdrew an exquisitely enameled gold box. In this she concealed her treasure. Dragging the chair across to the cupboards which ran the length of one wall, she climbed up and, by stretching on tiptoe, managed to push the box right to the back.

The task accomplished, her spirits lightened and vanity beckoned. The woman in her responded eagerly to those mirrors—from the beautiful oval one set on the table near the window to the others, full length and elegantly proportioned, placed strategically about the room.

Pilar had never before seen herself so often or so becomingly reproduced; with almost narcissistic compulsion she peered and preened and postured, snatching up the silver-backed brush from the table to burnish her hair with luxuriant, sweeping strokes, sliding the lord's ring once more onto her finger and extending her hand arrogantly to admire the heavily chased head.

Lightness of spirit was turning to heady excitement. What a fine lady she would make! It needed only a dress worthy of her new station in life, and there were dresses aplenty in the closets—evidence, if evidence be needed, of her husband's fancies! Pilar shrugged. Well, he might have all the mistresses he chose so long as he acknowledged her as wife.

Her toes encountered something incredibly soft; it was the finery laid out for her the previous night. It had slipped from the bed and now lay in a heap at her feet. Pilar lifted it. The silk warmed instantly to her touch as though it were alive—a tantalizing cobweb, spider-spun, clinging with a whispering softness against her skin. Never had she known anything so shameful . . . or so fine!

4

Fredericks moved quietly about the Viscount's room. The shades, discreetly drawn against the aggressive brilliance of the morning sunlight, cast a funereal gloom over an atmosphere already oppressive with heavy, somber furnishings. On this particular morning the effect seemed peculiarly apt.

The valet's ascetic features registered acute pain as an erratic, unharmonious concert of stentorian snores penetrated the thick hangings of the fourposter. Absentmindedly, but with a sureness born of long practice, he set about assembling the ingredients of a powerful, if unpalatable, restorative, the receipt for which was known only to himself. For once his hands were not quite steady.

In the ordinary way, Fredericks enjoyed coming to High Tor, here on the Yorkshire-Westmorland border, where, for the length of his stay, he was permitted to assume the exalted role of major domo. He had been Lord Gilmore's man for ten years, having taken up his post on the Viscount's seventeenth birthday, just before they had set out on the Grand Tour with Mr. Carvray. In that time, he'd seen his lordship through a fair number of scrapes, but nothing to equal this latest kick-up!

There had been women before, of course—regular little barques of frailty, some of them! But they had always known their place, and since Mrs. Verney had come on the scene, his lordship had scarcely looked at another woman. Hadn't been let, like as not! Perhaps that was the trouble, for when the cat's away . . . ! Fredericks permitted himself the driest semblance of a smile; he wouldn't mind being a fly on the wall when his lordship's mistress got wind of this latest caper!

The smile quickly faded, however, as he faced the unpalatable truth. His lordship, married to a . . . he couldn't bring himself to frame the word. Bridie had called her a foul-mouthed savage, who had driven her from the room with a stream of abuse ringing in her ears, but Bridie was a girl who laid herself open to abuse.

For his own part, that unexpected encounter in the corridor had affected him strangely—as though he had come upon a terrified, cornered wild animal. He'd half hoped she would cut and run—God forgive him, he had even done a little prompting in that direction—but she was still here, he could hear her moving about next door, so perhaps she was not deserving of his pity, after all.

A slight shudder shook Fredericks' neat frame. A gypsy! It didn't bear thinking about. He completed his preparations, walked soft-footed to the bed, and threw back the curtains. The Viscount didn't stir; he sprawled like one dead where he had collapsed earlier. A morbid urge to see the present situation resolved almost prompted the valet to precipitate matters with a well-aimed prod, but he thought better of his rashness and was about to turn away when the Viscount rolled onto his back with a hiccuping snort, groaned as though in his death throes, and lay inert again.

Fredericks, recognizing the involuntary ritual as

a prelude to the return of full, agonizing consciousness, moved back to his appointed task and began to blend and mix.

The subdued sounds of movement came to Theo from somewhere beyond the unspeakable noises thundering away inside his skull. He endeavored to pry stubborn eyelids apart and a thousand white-hot needles pierced his eyeballs. He buried them in hands that shook.

"Curse you, Fredericks! Must you creep about as though you were already attending my obsequies?"

"Forgive me, my lord. I was not aware that your lordship was . . . er, awake."

"I wish to God I were not!" Theo's abrupt laugh turned to a shuddering groan. "Hell and the Devil! Where's that infernal potion of yours? Quickly, I beg you, man—or I'm done for!"

Fredericks steered the glass into a groping hand. The Viscount swallowed and gasped as the remedy took the skin off his throat, setting his eyes watering.

He tried to recall the events of the previous night. Some dull card party surely? Thorpe Manor, that was it. No doubt they'd drunk pretty freely, but . . . "I'll tell you something, Fredericks—I don't visit Pocklington again in a hurry. His wine's not at all the thing; Sir Roger reckoned it was corked!"

"Very likely, sir." The valet's voice was noncommittal.

"Well, burn it, man—my mouth's like a cesspit! Have you ever known me so badly castaway?"

Fredericks, well aware that he was treading a path of considerable delicacy, chose his words with care, parrying the question with a question.

"Perhaps, my lord, the celebrations were of a somewhat . . . unusual nature?"

"What the devil's that supposed to mean?" The Viscount made a further desperate attempt at recall, massaging his temples with tentative fingers. His efforts produced nought beyond a bruising tenderness, and did little to remove an overriding presentiment of doom.

Curse it! That probably meant he was badly dipped . . . vingt-et-un . . . macao . . . deep basset? He gave up the struggle. Adam would know. Good old cousin Adam always knew. . . .

"I'm getting up," he announced decisively.

Fredericks eyed the door to the adjoining room, wilting slightly as the need to speak grew more pressing. Poker-faced, he handed the swaying Viscount into a black brocade robe, handsomely frogged and braided in gold, and found time even in this moment of crisis to reflect that one could forgive much in a young gentleman who displayed so well! No need to be padding the shoulders of *his* coats as Lord Forton's man was obliged to do, and though one might crave a shade more fullness in the calf, the overall effect was more than pleasing. If only as much might be said for his temper!

Favoring, in the end, an oblique approach, he ventured tentatively, "Will you be wishing to partake of breakfast with her ladyship, sir?"

Lord Gilmore sought the support of an adjacent bedpost. "Good God! I knew there was something badly amiss! Never tell me my stepmother is here?"

"No, indeed, my lord."

"Then stop talking in riddles, man. My head won't stand it."

There was nothing left now but plain speaking. "I was alluding to . . ." Here Fredericks faltered. ". . . to your bride, sir."

The Viscount was suddenly still. "My what?"

"Your bride, sir."

It was so quiet, the valet could hear his own heart thudding. Then, with deceptive gentleness, "I think you must be raving, Fredericks. I have no bride."

"No, sir." There was just the right degree of doubt. "Forgive me, my lord, but . . . you are not quite yourself! Could the . . . er, happy event have slipped your mind, perhaps? You seemed very definite when you returned earlier with your . . ." Here Fredericks swallowed. ". . . with the young person, sir."

Bloodshot eyes were boring into him. "And since when, dolt, have you heeded anything I might say in my cups?"

The question, couched in dulcet tones, did little to reassure Fredericks. When his lordship spoke all soft and silky like that—it was time to look out! Yet necessity obliged him to persevere.

"The circumstances were such, my lord . . . there seemed little room for doubt. In short, Mr. Carvray was good enough to confirm it to me, sir."

The unhappy valet waited for the storm to break about his head. But, for once, that mastery of vocabulary which had always commanded Fredericks' respect, if not his outright admiration, appeared to have deserted the Viscount. He looked momentarily stunned, then seemed to gather himself. In an awful silence, and with a face like Judgment Day, he strode to the door and flung it wide.

A dark figure preened before the mirrors in the sunlight. His vision was still painfully impaired, but he was sobering by the minute, shocked into sobriety by what appeared, at first glance, to be the familiar contours of his mistress.

"Suzanne!"

The figure spun around; a cloud of hair drifted and settled—straight, black, and gleaming—into a waist no bigger than a hand's span; almond-slanted eyes, sloe-black and bright with apprehension, stared fiercely back at him. The pale, diaphanous gown shivered revealingly and a matching peignoir was instantly snatched up and held tightly clasped to cover the girl's nakedness.

Theo's relief that he had not committed the cardinal indiscretion withered in the face of a more shattering discovery—the girl was a complete stranger.

"Who . . . are you?" He ground the words out with difficulty.

For a moment the girl seemed similarly incapable of speech. Then she flung her head back imperiously. "I am Pilar. Your wife, lord."

"Are you, by God! We'll see about that!" The fumes of alchohol still clouded his brain . . . but surely, her voice, strongly accented, was familiar? His fists, thrust deep in the pockets of his exotic robe, clenched and unclenched in a fury of uncertainty.

Pilar watched him nervously. The slanting sunlight fell mercilessly on the strong-boned face, emphasizing a heavy blue shadow of stubble running from cheekline to jaw and reducing the eyes to glittering slits. With his black hair in wild disarray, he looked more fearsomely gypsy than she.

He advanced and she stepped back, clutching the peignoir more tightly, pressing its soft fur trimming convulsively into the hollow of her throat. His hand shot out to grasp her chin urgently—and their fingers brushed, setting her pulses leaping.

"Your story had best be convincing," he said

harshly. "I have a short, sharp way with brazen young doxies who seek to importune me."

She frowned over the unfamiliar-sounding word. "I do not know what is importune, lord, but I *am* your wife. I have my lines from the padre to prove it."

"Dunwoody?"

"I think that was his name."

"Dunwoody married us?" For the first time an element of uncertainly entered his voice. It was not lost on Pilar; as he relaxed his grip slightly, she twisted free.

"Ha!" she cried. "You do not even remember what happens! Then I, Pilar, will tell you, so that you may know."

He winced and sank weakly onto the arm of a nearby chair. "You will, indeed—but quietly, I implore you!"

Her comprehending glance had little of sympathy in it. "Yes, you were very drunk!" she said bluntly. "So drunk that you forget, perhaps, the gypsies . . . the wedding celebrations . . . and the girl who danced for you?" The struggle for recollection was mirrored in his eyes. "The one for whom you made much trouble?" she persisted. "That girl was me, lord.

"And later? When you had taken me from my people . . ." The interrogation continued ruthlessly. ". . . Do you remember waking that poor padre to make him marry us? Oh, that was quite a wedding, I tell you . . . with your pretty friend singing lewd hymns and everyone set to quarreling!"

Theo's recollections hadn't progressed that far; they were still lingering over a mass of swirling figures, and one in particular—graceful, bewitching!

Vicious! The young savage had scratched him! He touched his face and found it tender.

"But . . . Godammit! Why did no one try to stop me?"

"*Madre de Dios!*" She flung back her head. "How we tried! The good padre . . . your kinsman, Mr. Carvray . . . we all implored you, but you would have none of it!"

The pieces were slipping into place; the girl was telling the truth, of course, but what, in the name of heaven, had Adam been about to let him court such folly?

"And so Dunwoody married us?" The question was, by now, purely rhetorical, but she seized on it, her voice contemptuous.

"Yes. Oh, not willingly, you understand—but you threaten him with ruin, and so he agrees!"

"Very well," he snapped. "I will see your proof—the lines of which you spoke."

"So that you may destroy them? Oh, no, lord! they are safe hidden. But I have this." Preserving her decency one-handed, she dragged the ring awkwardly from her finger and thrust it tauntingly under his nose. "See? And no, I did not steal it!"

He took the signet ring, weighing it in his hand while his mind grappled with the problem of how to extricate himself. The creature must go, of course,—if not willingly, then she would have to be bought off. He tossed the ring contemptuously back at her and it rolled unheeded between bare brown feet.

"You may keep it, an' you will," he said carelessly, getting up. "For the rest, Dunwoody will have to untie his damned officious knots. I ain't in the market for a wife, so you can dress and rejoin your brethren without further delay."

"No!" She grabbed at his sleeve and his own fingers closed hard on her wrist, forcing her to slacken her grip.

"What the devil does *no* mean?"

"It means no, lord—I will not go!"

"Don't be impertinent. You'll do as I say."

She attempted to twist from his grasp and in doing so, her hair swung forward for an instant, exposing her back. Theo drew a sharp breath and caught the hair as it swung back, coiling it like a silken rope around his fingers, tightening his grip until she cried out and slackened her hold on the wrap. The silky garment slithered into a heap at her feet and she was suddenly still, crimson with shame in the revealing nightgown, the only sound her hard-caught breath. In the mirror, their glances locked and hers blazed with a fury that only partly concealed her fear.

His own expression was inscrutable; distaste, disgust, and anger stirred in him at the sight of the red, raw weals across her back, overlaying other, fainter marks which bore witness to past beatings.

"I had forgotten," he muttered, half to himself. "Your uncouth chief. He should be flogged himself for such appalling desecration! I can almost forgive you your trickery." He released her hair, watching it fall in a rippling curtain to hide the ugliness. "*Almost*," he added softly. "But you go, nonetheless."

She spun around, and he could see her searching wildly for the words that would make him listen. "It was no trick! And besides . . ." Her glance flicked to the bed and the color rose hotly in her face. ". . . it is already too late, lord."

The inference was obvious. His lip curled. "You lie."

"Prove it!" she spat at him.

"Oh, no! I'm no raw halfling to be gulled so easily!"

The argument had set Theo's head pounding afresh. He groped among the, as yet undisturbed dregs of memory, eyes narrowed against aching eyeballs to take in the girl's taut figure—unviolated, of that he was near-certain. His wincing glance slid over the pristine whiteness of the bedsheets flung back, their unrumpled state suggesting a lack of use, and came finally to rest on the quilt heaped near the window.

"And where did this unlikely consummation take place, my fine would-be wife?" he drawled with lethal mockery. "Except in your imagination. For I'll wager anything you care to name that if I had laid so much as a finger on you, I should bear fresh scars to prove it!"

Her glance flew guiltily to his cheek, which still bore the evidence of her nails from the previous night. He smiled grimly. For the first time he glimpsed the ignominy of defeat in her lovely eyes. Surprisingly, he felt a pang of remorse, of pity, even. She was very young, after all, and had been ill-used by him.

The recollection made him say, less harshly, "Come now. Be thankful, child! It might have gone much worse with you. At least you will leave my house untouched, as you entered it—perhaps even a little plumper in the pocket to make matters right with your chief."

But his sympathy was spurned. Pilar was in no mood to cry quarter.

"How dare you! Do you think it so easy? That you can buy back your freedom? No, and no! I will not leave!" she declared passionately. "It is my

right to be here. Your Mr. Carvray will not permit
that you send me away!"

"Mr. Carvray does not have the ordering of affairs here," he snapped. "This house is mine and I
alone give the orders."

"And you order me to leave? Is that to be the
way of it?" Her voice was loaded with scorn. "So
this is the word of a Gilmore of which you boasted
to me!"

Theo was, by now, every bit as angry as she; to
have his honor called into question flicked him on
the raw. He flushed a dull red.

"Insolent baggage!" The words were ground out
through shut teeth. "What would you know of
honor? A fair bargain I would uphold to the death,
let me tell you! But to be rendered halfway insensible by your accomplices, with the aid of some nox-
ious brew, in order that you might gain your ends?
Oh, no! Such conduct absolves me from all responsibility!"

He was already at the door, not caring that her
frightened face streamed with silent tears, deaf to
the desperate pleading in her voice.

"It was not so! Oh, please, lord! I cannot go
back. They will not own me!"

"Too bad, for no more do I! You may all have
thought me easy prey, but I am no pigeon for your
plucking and so you may tell your friends!"

"Ah . . . h! You are odious . . . *insensato* . . .
filthy bastard. . . ."

The door slammed shut on the stream of lan-
guage, and an exquisite Sèvres vase, aimed at his
head, shattered into a thousand pieces against its
stout oak panels.

A moment later the door was pushed open again,
tentatively. A face, round-eyed, round-mouthed, its

snub nose liberally sprinkled with freckles, peered fearfully from the shattered procelain to the raging, arrogant gypsy with tear-bright eyes.

"*Madre de Dios!* This place abounds with strange people! Who gave you leave to come?" demanded the tempestuous vision, unaware of the awe she was arousing in a young breast pining for romance.

"I'm Amy Trubshawe, milady. Mrs. Shilton sent me, for to wait on you."

Pilar looked her over. "Well—you are better than that other one. To her I was less than the dirt beneath her feet." She moved restlessly. "You know what I am?"

"Y-yes'm." The snub-nosed maid looked half-fearful as Pilar flung away to stare out of the window. Amy's eye lit on the discarded wrap and she picked it up. "Happen you'd best put this on, milady; the morning air's reet chilly."

"What is this?" Her mistress turned slowly, as though coming back from a great distance. She brushed a hand across her eyes. "Oh, yes." And then, "No. I wish to dress. Will you help me, Amy Trubshawe?"

5

Adam Carvray was making a solitary breakfast when Theo stormed into the morning room. He eyed his disheveled cousin balefully before addressing himself once more to his plate.

"You look exactly as you deserve, my boy. I confess I hadn't expected to see you so soon, but it seems the Devil looks after his own."

Theo slumped into a chair. "Spare me the sermonizing." He lapsed into a sullen silence which lasted until his misery got the better of him. "I'm in the very deuce of a coil, coz!" He raised haggard eyes. "Why did you let me do it?"

Adam took the accusation in his stride. He carved himself a fresh slice of ham.

"Black coffee?" he suggested, with a hand already half-extended toward the coffee pot.

Theo glowered. "I'll take porter—and be damned!"

"As you please." Adam set it before him and considered Theo's *cri de coeur* afresh. "I can understand your distress, of course," he said with maddening calm. "But as for preventing your . . . er, indiscretions, I wish you will tell me sometime how I may accomplish such a feat when you have the bit so firmly between your teeth. I fear the task is quite beyond me, if last night is any test—indeed,

to say you were intractable would be to understate
the case!"

"You could have dragged me away by force."

"Of course!" The gentle voice was heavy with
irony. "An admirable solution! I wonder, now,
why I did not think of it myself?"

Theo flushed and stirred uncomfortably. "It
would have saved a damnably awkward situation.
As things stand now, I don't know what the devil
I'm to do."

"Nothing you can do, my boy, save make the
best of a bad job. I anticipated your orders, by
the way. The young stallion was delivered to the
gypsy camp at first light. With any luck, they will
already be on the road."

Theo sat up. "You mean . . . I must acknowledge the chit? Are you gone mad?"

"Not mad, Theo," Adam said quietly. "I admit I
am not happy—I would as lief the situation had not
arisen, but that having been said, right must be
done. Pilar received assurances, from you, from me,
from Dunwoody. There is no way those assurances
can be honorably withdrawn." He gave his young
cousin a look from under straight brows. "Last
night you were confident that you could make of
her a lady."

"Last night I was rendered halfway insensible
with some gypsy poison, and can hardly be held responsible . . ." Theo became aware that he had lost
Adam's attention. He was looking toward the door
and coming slowly to his feet. Theo shifted in his
chair, tankard in hand, and stared incredulously at
the figure framed in the open doorway.

The gown was intended for a figure of more
statuesque proportions. The heavily-brocaded,
hooped skirt sat so low on the hips that it trailed

the floor, and the bodice was more daringly décolleté than its designer had intended. Her hair was inexpertly scraped high and liberally adorned with feathers. The result was ludicrous, and yet oddly appealing—like a child dressed up for a masquerade!

Theo choked on an angry laugh. "Egad! Is this what you would have me present to the world as my Viscountess? Look at her, coz. 'Tis a joke!"

Color made two bright spots high on Pilar's cheekbones. She stood with head proudly held, but her eyes sought Adam's with ill-concealed anxiety. He greeted her with reassuring courtesy, frowning as Theo still sprawled obstinately in his chair, his brooding glance encompassing the girl's extraordinary costume. "And who, pray, gave you leave to make free with my property?"

She fingered the dress lovingly. "Your cupboards are filled with dresses, lord. Would you begrudge me one?"

"Yes, baggage, I would! And furthermore, let me tell you, I don't admire your taste. A lady don't come to breakfast in a ball gown, especially one that lays her open to unwelcome civilities. Why, even Cousin Adam is hard put to it not to ogle you!"

Pilar's color deepened painfully and one hand flew to the low-cut bodice.

"Theo! That will do!" Adam threw him a furious look and came forward to hand Pilar to a chair. "Allow me to tell you, Lady Gilmore, that you look most charming. Will you take breakfast?"

The title rang unfamiliarly in Pilar's ears, but she allowed herself to be led forward, her coltish grace impeded by the encumbering skirts. She stared entranced at the table, spread with more food than she had ever seen.

"I may have anything I wish?"

Adam smiled. "You have but to command, ma'am. A little of the cold roast beef? Or a slice of ham, perhaps . . . or does your fancy run to fried bacon and eggs?" He ignored Theo's snort of derision as Pilar's plate grew more and more heaped. "Now, will you drink coffee—or is tea more to your liking?"

Uncertain, she chose tea and began to eat quickly, using her fingers with a neat dexterity until not a morsel remained. Then she drew the back of her hand across her mouth with a sigh of satisfaction, made as though to wipe her fingers on her dress, and stilled them as Adam unobtrusively handed her a napkin. Self-consciously she scrubbed her face and hands and looked up to find Lord Gilmore's eyes on her, full of mocking derision.

"The very acme of gentility!" he drawled. He sat forward suddenly and stabbed a finger at her. "Don't imagine for one moment that you have outsmarted me, young woman—and don't think to hide behind my cousin's coat skirts, either! He may fancy he can bear-lead me, but I *am* master in my own house, as you shall all discover presently." His voice hardened. "So if you have finished your breakfast—out you go!"

Pilar's hand trembled as she laid down the crumpled napkin. She threw Adam a silent, beseeching look.

For answer, he leaned forward calmly. "Will you take a little more tea, my lady? Another slice of bread and butter, perhaps? No? Then I suggest we repair to the yellow salon where we shall be a good deal more comfortable." He rose from his chair. "Permit me to apologize for your husband's execrable manners. He is seldom at his best before noon, particularly when he has overindulged himself the previous night. You may not credit as much, but he has great charm when he cares to exercise it."

"I warn you, coz—you go too far!" growled Theo.

Adam came behind him and said in a low voice, "I think not. Theo—be reasonable, I beg you. Like it or not, you all but forced the child into her present predicament. You cannot toss her back like a spent fish because she does not now measure up to your expectations."

"Can I not?" Theo looked up from smoldering contemplation of his red morocco slippers to view his wife. She, too, had risen and stood, a mixture of defiance and uncertainty, the fine gown slipping from one shoulder, the brave edifice of her hair in imminent danger of collapse; already one feather teetered comically over her ear. The feather was his undoing. His lips twitched uncontrollably, and without warning he dissolved into peals of laughter.

Pilar was well used to anger; with an effort born of long years of practice she could even swallow insults. But to be laughed at—this was insupportable!

She flew at Theo in a rage. He caught her flailing arms and jerked her forward until she was forced to her knees with her hands imprisoned against his chest, his face very close to hers.

"If you would be a lady," he said softly, "you must needs subdue that wild temper of yours."

She was suddenly still, blinking the mists of fury from her sloe-black eyes. "You mean . . . ?"

"I mean that maybe—just maybe—I will try my

hand at turning my sow's ear into a fine silk purse, after all."

Her fury melted magically into laughter. "Lord!" she cried passionately. "I will make you proud of me. You will see how quickly I will learn!"

Theo's brows rose. He glanced quizzically at his cousin. "Well, Adam? Does the notion please you?"

Adam looked thoughtful. "If you are indeed serious. . . ."

"Why not? My dear coz—I'll venture a wager on it, if you doubt me! Give me time and I'll transform her. Six months and she'll pass in any company. What do you say to that, baggage? You may yet end up a credit to your father, whoever he is!"

"That one!" Pilar spat the words vehemently. "No! I will kill him if he ever reveals himself to me!"

"You will do nothing of the kind. I'll brook none of your tantrums!" Theo's fingers tightened into bands of steel as her lower lip jutted obstinately. "I mean it, brat, so understand me well. Give me trouble and I wash my hands of you!" He gave her a little shake. "If, on the other hand, you are a good, obedient child and mind what I tell you—and what Mr. Carvray tells you—we might succeed in making you the toast of the town. The choice is yours."

Pilar shrugged—and then, unexpectedly, she grinned. "Yes, lord—I choose. And I will be quite splendid, you will see. Only tell me what you require me to do."

Theo raised her to her feet and found that the ache in his head had all but gone. "Well, for one thing, you can stop addressing me as 'lord.' Theo will suffice—or Gilmore—or, my lord, if you must. And you can go and remove that ridiculous costume. A dressmaker must be found to fashion you some kind of wardrobe to go on with. I assume there will be dressmakers, even in this benighted spot . . . someone discreet. Fredericks will know."

"You mean to stay here for the present, then?" Adam asked.

"Oh, I think we must—for a few days, at least. Can't risk removing her to Ashenden until she's reasonably rigged out and we've knocked off a few of the rough edges."

Pilar looked from one to the other, simmering with indignation. "I am not a lump of clay! I do not have rough edges! As for dresses, there are a great number of them upstairs. I could make them to fit."

"No!" Theo said with unwarranted curtness.

"They are for your woman. I know that," she said, with that frankness which he was beginning to find disconcerting. "But so many! She would not miss . . ."

"Don't be impertinent!" he snapped, while Adam's lips twitched.

"Then tell me," she demanded, undaunted, "am I to wear my own clothes until this dressmaker is found? Or do you wish that I wrap myself in a blanket meanwhile?"

Adam chuckled. "The child has a valid point, Theo."

"Very well. One dress, and *I* will choose it," Theo said furiously. "And, in future, pray do as you are bid without argument!"

Pilar shrugged and turned, muttering, to the door. There she encountered Sir Roger. If Lord Gilmore had presented a ramshackle appearance on rising, it was as nothing to his friend. Gone was the exquisite; an exotically embroidered banyan in yellow silk served only to emphasize Sir Roger's unhealthy pallor, and without his toupee his sandy hair stood up in spikes, making him appear oddly boyish.

He pulled up short, an expression of acute horror crossing his face. Instinct prompted him to make her an elegant leg, but it was patently obvious from the groping desperation in his eyes that he had not the smallest recollection of her.

Theo enlightened him, enjoying the sight of his friend, for once, at a loss for words. Sir Roger bowed again, stammering awkwardly. Pilar caught sight of bare shanks and embroidered yellow morocco slippers with ridiculous curling toes. She swallowed a wild urge to laugh and returned his salutation with an inelegant bob.

"Not like that, child! Not like that!" Theo groaned. "You are aspiring to be a lady, not a scullery maid!"

It was the first of many cutting reprimands she was to incur over the weeks that followed, for the Viscount proved a harshly demanding taskmaster. Tempers flared often. For all her fine promises, Pilar was often intractable, finding the restrictions placed upon her to be irksome, wildly unreasonable—and even frightening. Used all her life to roaming at will, she bitterly resented the Viscount's demands on her time—the constant vigilance.

It was like housing a smoldering volcano; doors and windows were constantly flung wide and raised voices often preceded the crash of hurled crockery—a situation calculated to unsettle everyone in that hitherto masculine residence.

But she learned too—developing a splendid air of

hauteur and showing an aptitude for mimicry shamelessly exploited by Sir Roger (whom she christened Sir Ham, being unable to get her tongue around his name), who found the whole affair hugely diverting.

Discreet inquiries had yielded a seamstress from a nearby village—a surprisingly competent little woman who came equipped with a comprehensive selection of up-to-the-minute fashion plates, together with a length of rose brocade and another of striped tabby silk left on her hands by a client.

Her first and most urgent task was to make over a dress of bright yellow damask to fit Pilar, an exercise which proved horrifyingly uncomfortable for the girl—even Amy's envious sighs and the compliments of Sir Roger and Mr. Carvray failed to reconcile her. After two days of misery, she seized the first opportunity which offered to slip through the gap in the wall of the kitchen garden and into the field beyond.

With the joy of being free, she picked up her skirts and ran through the tall grasses, where the bracken was turning golden, toward the sound of water.

She tugged impatiently at the jonquil ribbons confining her elegant straw bergère hat, and in a small copse near the river's edge she flopped down in the shelter of a clump of elders and cast the offending hat into the air; the breeze caught and lifted it and deposited it with scant respect on a nearby bush.

Next to go were the dainty yellow shoes—and finally, she peeled off the hateful stockings and lay back with her eyes shut, wriggling her toes blissfully in the cool grass.

The river burbled comfortably in the background, a lazy sound blending harmoniously with the drone of a bee still lingering drowsily over memories of high summer days. There were scufflings and cheepings in the branches above her and a dry whisper brought a leaf floating prematurely to land on her face.

Pilar brushed it away and sighed despondently. It was no use—she could not be comfortable. Nothing had been as she had imagined; she was no longer sure if she could submit to the rigors of being made into a lady—for no one had told her about stays which laced so tightly that one could scarcely breathe! The splendid notions of taking her rightful place in the world and thus spiting that noble *Gorgio* who had spawned her with so little thought, faded before the misery of stays—and of having every waking hour ordered and supervised. Above all else, one must behave!

She rolled rebelliously onto her stomach and peered over the jutting riverbank; in a crystal clear pool, three trout hovered motionless, their rhythmically moving gills the only sign of life. Pilar's eyes sparked into life. She pushed up the priceless mechlin lace of her sleeve and slid a hand into the pool with infinite care . . .

And that was how Theo found her—at full stretch, her face wiped clean of all expression, legs exposed to the knee, with one foot pointing rigidly skyward, its toes curled tight.

For one terrible moment he thought her dead, or at the very least in a near-fatal swoon. He heard with awful clarity Adam's admonition that he was riding her too hard.

But even as he was cursing his own intolerance, there was a spasm in the foot—her arm came up with a sudden jerk and something black and gold and shining came curving through the air; a nine-inch trout lay flapping at his feet and Pilar rolled over and sat up with a squeak of triumph which turned to a keening wail as she saw him for the first time.

In that instant she was all gypsy—tumbled and disheveled, but vitally alive as she had not been since the night he had brought her home. The realization only served to fan his anger.

"Get up!" He strode forward and hauled her, protesting, to her feet. "How dare you behave so ... abominably! What, in the name of heaven, do you suppose you are about?"

Pilar hid her dismay behind a stubbornly set jaw. "I am tired of doing what you tell me. Today, I do what I want."

"The devil you do! We made a bargain, my fine wife. Is this how you keep it? With a display of outright disobedience?"

"I do not wish to disobey, but you talk and talk and you don't comprehend at all how it is for me. Do you know what it is to wear stays? No! Well, I will endure *them* if I must, but how would you support having to sit for long hours stupidly plying a needle and being lectured by an ill-tempered husband who says, 'Do not run,' 'Do not laugh aloud,' 'Do this,' 'Do that' ... and so on and on! I have to get away!"

"Ill-tempered, is it?" The accusation rankled. "Let me tell you, I have been amazingly forbearing in the circumstances. Dammit, you *have* to learn! How else are you to take your place convincingly? I have explained it all a score of times. I had thought by now that even you would understand!"

"And I think that you might understand how

sometimes I feel suffocated. I am not used to houses. I need to be alone—to be free."

Theo made a gesture of exasperation. "That's all very fine, but suppose one of my keepers had come upon you as I did just now?"

Pilar tossed her head and loosed a pin, bringing a cluster of hair cascading about her shoulders. "I should have made myself known to him, of course."

"Egad! I'd give a monkey to see his face." Theo cast a ruthless eye over her. "My dear green girl, he would have laughed in your face . . . probably ravished you on the spot! Do you imagine Milady Gilmore would ever be found lying on her stomach tickling trout with her hair in disarray and her face streaked with dirt?"

She put up a hand to scrub guiltily at her cheek and made matters worse.

Theo groaned. "Enough! We had best admit here and now that the task is an impossible one. You are simply not comfortable! Come back to the house and we will decide what must be done."

"Oh, no!" Pilar's heart gave a great lurch of dismay. She flew to scoop up her stockings and, after a moment's uncertainty, rolled them into a ball, stuffed them down her bodice and thrust her feet into the now damp yellow satin slippers. "I will learn, I promise! And I will try to be good and obedient . . . and oh!" She seized the hat from its incongruous perch and crammed it back on her head. "Oh, I beg you, do not send me away!"

Theo took the ribbons from her fumbling fingers and tied them expertly beneath her chin. She stared up at him, tears beading the thick sweep of her lashes. A stifled sniff of pure desolation escaped her. It was his undoing.

"Undoubtedly I should have held to my resolve," he told Adam later. "But dammit, she suddenly looked for all the world like that runt out of Bessie's litter . . . d'you remember? The one we hid from Pa that summer when I was home with an inflammation of the lungs?"

"I remember," said Adam, smiling. "I also remember what happened to that runt. It turned out to be the pick of the bunch!"

And so Pilar submitted with something less than a good grace to the ministrations of Miss Pym, allowing herself to be pinned and prodded and twitched into reluctant elegance under the rigorously watchful eye of the Viscount.

The seamstress was astonished, and not a little shocked, by his lordship's intimate knowledge of the details governing a lady's toilet, but she pursed her lips and reflected that the gentry were a law unto themselves. There had been talk in the village of other . . . females at High Tor, one in particular, as fair and lovely as this young bride was dark and strange! There had been talk about her, too, but Miss Pym closed her mind to it; after years of making dresses for unlovely, ungrateful women, she had the chance at last to advance her reputation. If the Viscount approved her work, there might be further commissions.

And Pilar, like a butterfly newly emerged from its chrysalis, stood a little in awe of her new self. Almost without her knowing it, her metamorphosis had begun.

6

"It is time you gave serious consideration to the engaging of a suitable companion for Pilar," Adam said. "It is neither right nor desirable that she should be constantly in the company of men. She would derive much greater benefit from the society and conversation of some gently raised female."

"No!" cried husband and wife simultaneously.

They were seated on the terrace at Ashenden in the mellow autumn sunshine. Ashenden stood on the fringe of Epsom. Pilar had loved it on sight for its welcome air of spaciousness, and perhaps a little because, like her, it was a bit of a mongrel. In essence a gracious, creeper-covered sixteenth-century manor house, it had been subjected to the fashionable whim of the Fourth Viscount and now stood flanked by a pair of Gothic octagonal towers.

Pilar's bedchamber was situated in the west tower, delighting her with three deep-set windows, each fashioned with comfortable cushioned seats and each offering a new prospect of park and woodland with here and there a glint of water, the domed minaret of a hidden gazebo—and in the far distance, the rolling downs.

Here, for the first time, she began to feel herself a lady; the servants accepted her as such; and if they thought her eccentric—well, she was, after all,

a foreigner! Only Fredericks and Amy Trubshawe
had traveled with them from Yorkshire, and both
could be trusted to keep their council.

"The fewer people we involve at this stage, the
better," Theo stated positively.

"And for me, I do not like women," Pilar added.
"Besides, I do not need anyone. Amy Trubshawe is
my good friend and looks after me very well. For
the rest," here she wrinkled her nose deprecia-
tingly, "I have my lord who instructs me in the
way I must conduct myself—and you, dear Mr.
Carvray, who will teach me to read and to write,
and extend to me your so good advice. Is this not
enough?"

Adam smiled. "I think not, my dear. Believe me,
you would do so much better with some suitable
lady. Amy is, after all, but a servant. . . ."

"I do not regard such things!"

"Then you should," he reproved gently.
"Preserve your good relationship with Amy by all
means—but as mistress and maid only. You will not
learn those niceties of conversation, behavior, and
judgment so necessary to you from Amy." He
looked to Theo for support.

"Quite right. I am always telling you, you're a
sight too familiar with the servants!"

"Meecham likes me."

"Of course, he likes you, puss," Sir Roger said la-
zily from the depths of an ample cane chair. "You
have a way of making folk like you, and your esteemed butler is no exception. Why, you've had
Fredericks around your little finger since the night
he gave notice."

"Don't exaggerate, Ham" said Theo tersely, not
wishing to be reminded how narrowly tragedy had
been averted.

It had all arisen out of a trifling incident—in those very early days, an argument between Pilar, Miss Pym, he and Amy. In a rush of exasperation, Theo had summoned Fredericks.

"For God's sake, man, set these women straight! How is her ladyship's hair best dealt with?"

Fredericks had assumed a wooden expression; a very faint flush ran up under his skin. "With respect, my lord—I believe you will agree that there is very little I would refuse your lordship." His nostrils quivered. "But turn lady's maid, I will not—even for you, sir."

The Viscount was stunned. "You'll damned well do as I ask—or find yourself another place."

The flush had died away, leaving the valet very pale. "As you wish, my lord." He coughed nervously. "Lord Forton has approached me on more than one occasion. Of course, it would grieve me greatly to leave your lordship's service."

"Forton! The Devil! How dare he! Don't be a blithering idiot, man—Forton would drive you to Bedlam in a week!"

Fredericks made no answer, though his prim features registered vague distress. The situation had seemed incapable of resolution, and then Pilar had touched the valet's neat, black-clad arm.

"Mr. Fredericks," her tongue stumbled awkwardly over his name. "You know well that my lord would be desolate without you." She smiled and her eyes were dark, seeming to bewitch him. "And you also, I think. So, can we not make a bargain, you and I? I quite see that what Lord Gilmore asks is, for you, an affront to your dignity, but perhaps if you would consent to impart to Amy a little of your so very great experience, she would be most quick to learn. . . ."

Capitulation had been surprisingly swift. Theo had been a little annoyed to find his dry, imperturbable valet so susceptible to his wife's gypsy wiles. Fredericks' judgment had been impeccable, as always; none of the absurd erections decreed by fashion, he'd insisted, but a style based on severely classical lines to set off milady' magnificent hair to advantage and compliment her beautiful high cheekbones. And perhaps, on occasion, a Spanish comb—a mantilla?

Sir Roger's drawl broke his train of thought. "Do I not get a mention in your list of mentors, puss?"

Theo snorted. "What would Pilar learn from a frippery fellow like you?"

"Address, my boy," murmured the beau, unabashed. "A Baronet may not rank with a Viscount, but I fancy I may have the edge when it comes to those little touches so necessary to set one apart from the commonplace."

Pilar came to hang with forbidden laxity over the back of his chair. "You are very fine, I think, but you make me laugh."

"That for you, my lad," said Adam with a chuckle.

"I refuse to be cast down. A genius is oft reviled in his own country."

"Oh, but I do not revile you. I enjoy to laugh." Pilar cast a look of defiance at her lord. "I have not laughed nearly enough until now." A wheedling note crept into her voice. "And there is something you can do for me, if you will. . . ."

"I thought there'd be a catch!" Sir Roger eyed her suspiciously. "What maggot's eating you, now?"

"Can you shoot with a pistol?"

"Gracious, child!" Adam looked shocked. "Whatever next? You never want to learn to shoot!"

"I might. What is so wrong?"

"Out of the question," Theo said curtly.

"I do not see why," she complained. "I have been most willing to learn any number of disagreeable things. Why should I not be allowed just one of my own choosing?"

"No reason at all, if you choose sensibly. But pistol-shooting is not a young lady's pursuit."

" 'Tis an unusual one, I grant you." Sir Roger, in a fit of quixotic perversity, supported Pilar. "But that's because most of 'em would succumb to the vapors on the spot! Not like our Pilar, eh?" She sent him a shining look. "It could be a handy trick to have up her sleeve at that, with damned footpads and the like! But it's not me you want, *querida*," he confided, ignoring Theo's black frown. "Theo's your man. I've seen him put out a candle flame at thirty paces without disturbing the wax. I wouldn't care to call him out, I can tell you!"

"Really?" Pilar turned her considering gaze on her husband. "Have you killed a great number of men, lord?"

"Certainly not!" said Theo tersely. "Ham, stop being provoking."

"Nothing of the kind. You are too modest, Theo!" Sir Roger was, by now, in an irrepressible mood. "Oh, your husband's a terrible fellow, Pilar. He's almost as deadly with a sword—graduated from the Fives Court Academy as one of Harry Angelo's prize pupils!"

"Ham, for God's sake be still!" warned Adam, only too aware that Pilar was becoming infected by his foolery.

She swaggered across to Theo now, swinging her hips provocatively. "But can you throw a knife, lord?" she challenged.

"No, I cannot. And I will thank you not to walk like a common strumpet! Sit down."

"I will make you a bargain, lord," she said, undeterred by his brusqueness. "You will teach me to shoot a pistol and I will show you how to throw the knife. Yes?"

"No, I thank you," he said repressively. "I have no wish to add knife-throwing to my list of accomplishments."

"Then forgive me, but you are a fool. A knife is fast, and kills silently—not like your pistol, which makes much noise." Her eyes grew bright with anticipation. "We could make a contest, you and I—and I will prove it to you."

"We will do nothing of the kind!" said Theo with finality. "It may come as a disappointment to you, little savage, but others do not share your apparent partiality for killing people! So we will have no more talk of pistols or knives, if you please. The only skill I would have you display with a knife is at the table. Now, you will sit down and recite for me please, in correct order of precedence, the Princes and Princesses of the Blood Royal, with their correct titles, as I have taught you. . . ."

"How is it that you bear with my lord?" Pilar demanded of Adam later. "Sir Roger I can understand; they are something alike. But you are so very different, and yet you have an affection for him, I think."

Adam sighed ruefully. "He does make it a little difficult sometimes, but the fault is not entirely his." Pilar looked skeptical, and after a moment he said, "Perhaps you should know something of our background; it might help you understand Theo a little better.

"I was adopted somewhat grudgingly by my uncle—Theo's father—when my own parents died, before Theo was born. His mother and mine had been sisters, and she became like a second mother to me. A gentle creature, but delicate—she survived Theo's entry into the world by no more than a few hours."

Pilar made a small, distressed sound.

Adam smiled. "Little boys are surprisingly resilient. My uncle was not a . . . lovable man, so small wonder that my starved affections turned to Theo. . . ."

"I should think you would have hated him," exclaimed Pilar. "His birth took your aunt from you, did it not?"

"True. And I think at the outset I was prepared to do so, but he won my heart instantly and I resolved to love and protect him for always. And wayward though he has been all his life, I have never regretted that childish resolve. I like to think that I have enjoyed a certain amount of affection in return, though it may not always be evident."

"He is more fortunate than he deserves," protested Pilar.

"You think so now, child. But his early years were desperately lonely. I was away at school much of the time and his father married again. With the best will in the world I can find little good to say of Theo's stepmother. She is, and always was, a cold, charmless woman who cared nothing for him. In due course she produced two daughters, and upon these she has lavished what little feeling she possesses. In consequence, Theo grew to manhood unpredictable, restless, and cynical beyond his years." Adam patted Pilar's hand. "But, though it takes a little finding, there is yet something of his mother's sweetness in him."

Pilar was hard pressed to find it as her education continued at a rigorous pace; only in her dancing, it seemed, did she come anywhere near to pleasing him, quickly mastering the minuet and cotillion, performing with spirit and grace.

She was made to practice curtsies of varying depth over and over, and to learn to whom each was due. Even mealtimes were not exempt, as she was initiated into the complexities of etiquette governing the dinner table—when one might converse across the board and when this was forbidden.

Her head began to reel with the number of facts it was expected to retain, and without Sir Roger to buoy her up with his infectious gaiety, and Adam Carvray's quiet encouragement, she must have rebelled more often than she did.

They both voiced their disapproval, for it seemed that no matter how hard she tried, the Viscount remained critical. If he found her laughing over some triviality with Sir Roger, he scowled, and in consequence some imp of perversity made her behave the more outrageously when he was near.

Inevitably, matters came to a head. On a morning when the skies were too overcast to encourage outdoor pursuits, Adam was seated before the fire reading. Theo was temporarily absent and Pilar and Sir Roger, seizing their chance, were at a nearby table throwing the dice in a friendly squabbling way, like children; when he accused her roundly of cheating and took out his snuff box, the game lapsed and they fell instead to talking about snuff, its flavors and methods of usage. These were sur-

prisingly comprehensive and his lordship presently
entered the room to find Pilar, her hand extended
provocatively toward Sir Roger. . . .

"Now then, m'dear—the idea is for the gentleman
to place a pinch on your dainty wrist, and then,
d'you see, he takes your hand, and raises it so."

She giggled. "But it tickles! Do ladies do this often?"

"Ladies do not do it at all!" They had not heard
the door open, but now it slammed shut and Theo
strode forward, his face thunderous. "Ham—you'll
oblige me by not teaching my wife to affect the
manners of a demi-rep!"

Slightly shamefaced, Sir Roger took a liberal
pinch of snuff, snapped his box shut, and dusted his
kerseymere waistcoat. "Oh, come now, dear boy!
A harmless, flirtatious device, no more. Why, 'tis a
trick I have seen you employ more than once!"

The revelation did nothing for Theo's temper.
"For God's sake, man—use the sense you were born
with! What you or I might do in certain company
is not pertinent here. Pilar is incorrigible enough already."

"You are being less than just, Theo," said Adam
mildly.

"Yes, you are!" insisted Pilar.

"Am I?" He swung around on her. "Then tell
them where I found you this very morning . . . on
your knees in the stable, mixing some wretched
poultice and lecturing Potter on its correct applica-
tion!"

"Oh, lor!" murmured Sir Roger ruefully.

"What is so wrong? I know this paste—I have
made it many times. It will cure Prince's strained
hock—you will see! There is nothing the Romany
does not know about horses."

"Or about people, it seems. Not only are you on familiar terms with every stable hand, plying your dratted 'cures,' but I now find that you extend a similar service to my kitchens!"

There was a muffled laugh from Sir Roger, and Adam frowned.

"It was only the cook," Pilar explained defensively. "She had *the screws* something dreadful, Amy said, and so I told her what to do. Why should she go on suffering when I have the means to relieve her?"

"Heaven give me patience! How many times must I say it, Pilar? Forget your past!"

Pilar sprang to her feet, hands on hips. "You would have me deny my Romany blood?"

"Yes, I would! If we are to believe your fictions, you were never more than half gypsy, so it should not be beyond you. Time grows short. You will have to start meeting people very soon, and I am far from being satisfied with you. Perhaps, if you would direct your misplaced energies to your appointed tasks, we might achieve better results!"

"For shame!" cried Sir Roger.

"Children!" Adam protested. "What a quarrelsome pair you are, to be sure! Theo—you are being grossly unfair. Pilar has worked extremely hard and has come on superbly."

"Indeed I have! And it has not been easy, let me tell you, with such a one as you to please!" She glared, before turning to sweep Adam a curtsy of just the right depth, head proudly held, hand extended. "There!" she declared. "Is not this well done?"

"Exquisitely so, my lady." Adam took her hand with a smile, carried it to his lips, and raised her up.

"Oh, very pretty!" said Theo sarcastically.

"What a pity you do not take such pains when I demand the same of you!"

"You answer yourself out of your own mouth, lord." Pilar's eyes flashed dangerously. "You *demand*. Sir Ham and Mr. Carvray, you see, always treat me as a lady—and so I feel a lady. Perhaps you might care to try this some time. You would be surprised, I think!"

The door slammed shut behind her.

"Insolent baggage!" Theo fumed. "You see what I mean? Deliberately provoking. Dammit, she's getting above herself. Mayhap, it's another kind of lesson she needs!"

Sir Roger strolled toward the door himself, observing with less than his customary good humor, "I am open to correction, of course, but it would seem to me that there has been too much of *that* in her young life already! And if you will take a piece of advice, Theo—you will tread carefully. The child is an original! Don't crush her spirit by endeavoring to make her over into a pale imitation of Suzanne!" He bowed formally. "Adam—I am at your disposal. When you are free, perhaps you will ride over with me to Colonel Wraxton's to take a look at that gelding of his."

"Ham presumes too much on friendship," snapped Theo. "When I want his advice, I'll ask for it!"

"You don't think perhaps he might be right?" Adam's voice was carefully noncommittal. "Pilar has great freshness and charm. Ask too much of her and you are in danger of destroying it. Trouble is, you are too alike—both self-willed and stubborn! Ease up on her, Theo—be a little kind. It will work wonders."

But Theo did not feel kind; he felt even less so

when he reached the stables to find that his wife had ridden out before him. It did not need the sheepish glances accompanying the information to tell him that she had violated his wishes yet again.

Pilar had gone straight to her room and changed her dress for a riding habit of vibrant green velvet, helped by Amy who, having taken one hasty glance at her mistress's face, was by now wise enough to hold her peace.

The same held good in the stables and she was soon riding at breakneck pace across the fields and up toward the high ridge beyond Gilmore land. Forbidden territory! The thought exhilarated her, drove her on. Unencumbered by a saddle, the horse's body between her legs gave her a comfortable feeling of belonging. The rising wind was blowing a fine mizzle into her face. She flung her head up, reveling in the feel of it on her skin like a benediction, soothing away the worst of her anger.

A horseman cantering along the ridge saw her coming, and drew rein. Without making the least push to intervene, he watched the headlong gallop, as a predator might watch its intended victim; as if on cue, a pheasant flew up almost at the horse's feet, causing the frightened animal to shy violently and slither out of control.

Only as the skirt billowed out, did he realize that the unseated rider was a girl. He spurred his hunter and arrived in time to hear a stream of unladylike invective, delivered in a curious mixture of English, Spanish, and some other, unrecognizable tongue.

He dismounted swiftly and set about untangling the struggling, furious girl.

"Unhand me, senor!" she demanded, attempting to rise and groaning as her body protested at the unwarranted assault upon its bruised parts. "I am not broken, I assure you."

"One moment, ma'am—if you will permit me!" The gentleman, highly diverted, leaned forward to extricate the chain of a medallion which had become stubbornly enmeshed in her hair. He glanced at it as it came free. His hand stilled and he looked closer; then he calmly completed his task and set it around her neck again with a certain precision.

"A pretty trinket," he said casually. "A family heirloom, no doubt?"

"It was my mother's," she said absently, all her attention on the little mare. Having tasted freedom, Mayfly was ambling back, stopping here and there to nibble at a bush. Pilar watched anxiously, ready to detect the slightest trace of a limp. Theo would never forgive her if Mayfly should have suffered any damage! She knelt to run a hand expertly over the mare's hocks, watched with some interest by her rescuer.

"There is no tenderness." She sighed, and stood up. "Thank you for your help, senor. If you would assist me now to mount?"

So he was to receive his congé? He eyed the mare's back, bare of saddle, and she adopted an air of hauteur to cover her embarrassment. He cupped his hands and she vaulted lightly up and settled herself astride the mare, quickly arranging her skirts.

At the last, he laid a restraining hand on the bridle. "Am I to know whom I have had the pleasure of serving?"

Pilar thought of Theo. How he would be enraged if he knew of this encounter! She wished now that she had not ridden so far. This gentleman was of a manner most personable, with his light brown hair and cool, amused gray eyes that missed very little and made her feel discomforted! It would not do for him to know her name.

So she smiled down and said, conspiratorially, "I think not, senor. It is so much more exciting just to be strangers. You understand?"

His comprehensive look said only too plainly that he did, but he acquiesced with a good grace and let her go.

She was scarcely back on Gilmore land when she saw Theo coming very fast. She veered away, but he had soon drawn level and had her rein tight held.

He dismounted and hauled her unceremoniously from the horse's back, in spite of her vehement protests.

"Save your breath," he advised curtly. "You are going to need it."

Pilar pulled away, her eyes flashing. "I do not know what you intend, but . . ." She watched him mount and move away, leading Mayfly behind him. "What are you doing?"

"Why—since you so obviously feel the need of exercise, the walk back will do you good . . . give you the opportunity to indulge that desire for freedom which seems to weigh so much with you!"

"But . . . we are miles from home! And it mizzles!" She ran, flinging the words at his retreating back. "You cannot leave me here!"

Theo was crossing the hall when she was finally admitted by a stolid footman. A film of mist beaded her habit; it glistened on her hair, her eyelashes. Her hat hung limply in her hand, trailing a miserable feather, but her eyes blazed.

"How dare you treat me so!"

For answer, he strode across to the salon and flung the door wide. "In here!"

She tossed her head. "I am wet, and tired from all that walking. I wish to change my habit."

"My heart bleeds! Now—in here."

Pilar flounced past him and stood in the middle of the room, a shoulder hunched against him. He regarded her coldly.

"We must have a reckoning, you and I. You once expressed a desire to be a grand lady. We made a bargain . . . and perhaps you feel that you have honored it. If so, you are amazingly naive— which I very much doubt! You have certainly succeeded in wrapping Sir Roger and Adam around your fingers! But there is a trait in your character which is totally unconformable, and I am no longer prepared to tolerate your constant flouting of my directions!"

"And I have told you!" she retorted, turning to face him. "Me—I would be a most excellent pupil if you would only treat me as human, instead of barking orders at me as if I were your puppy dog!"

"Not a dog, my dear," he said softly. "A bitch! A tiresome little mongrel bitch!"

She sprang at him, but he caught her hands before they reached his face.

"Oh, no! You don't do that twice! I've a mind to mend your manners for you, once and for all!"

"Ha!" She taunted him. "So you would resort to beating, after all, lord? For all your fine words, you are no better than Fergus Lovell!"

"I now appreciate the provocation that man must have had!" Theo said with feeling. "And nothing would give me greater pleasure at this moment, be-

lieve me, than to take a whip to you, but that
would provide no more than a temporary gratifica-
tion of my feelings. I'd do better to discover the
whereabouts of your reprehensible brethren and return you to their fold, forthwith! With my
blessing!"

He felt her go rigid with shock. "You cannot do
that! I am your wife!"

"In name only—and not for much longer, I
promise you," he swept on recklessly. "I'll do what
I should have done in the beginning—have the marriage annulled."

Madre-de-Dios! He meant it! The words grew
thick in her throat. "But . . . you cannot!"

"You think not? Well, we shall see, my wife!"

"You . . . are trying to frighten me . . ."

He said nothing. She wrenched herself free.

"I will not go back!" she cried passionately. "I
. . . I will kill myself if you try to make me!"

"Good!" he declared with grim satisfaction.
"That will save me the trouble of an annulment!"

She stared at him, wild-eyed, and rushed from
the room. He swore savagely and spent the next
two hours working his hunter into a lather. And
came home in a worse humor than when he had
left.

7

When Pilar failed to appear at dinner, Theo assumed she was sulking in her room and resolved harshly that she should stay there—but with both Adam and Sir Roger out, he was reduced to dining alone, and found it a dismal experience. Try as he might to fan the flame of grievance against Pilar, by his third glass of port he was obliged to admit that he missed her.

He had grown used to her chatter and was remembering the number of times she had made him laugh. His fourth glass induced such clarity of mind that he was taking upon himself at least a part of the blame for their frequent clashes of will. Why had it become such a matter of pride with him to make Pilar over to his liking? By the end of the second bottle, he was no nearer answering the question—but it no longer mattered. He had discovered that he wanted her just the way she was, temper and all!

In her room he found only Amy, who hadn't seen milady since she had gone riding earlier. She stared uneasily at the rain-streaked windows; the daylight had almost gone. Inquiries were discreetly initiated by Meecham. No one had seen Lady Gilmore that afternoon. The house was searched to no avail. Mayfly was still in the stable, so she hadn't run away. Besides, where would she go?

Theo's heart was pounding uncomfortably as he sprinted toward the nearest of the park's three meres. The rain was driving steadily in his face, and with every step her voice drummed in his head . . . "I will kill myself if you try to make me. . . ."

A willow tree, now bare of leaf, trailed tangled stems across the surface of the water, gently undulating, like lifeless strands of hair.

He found her close by, a forlorn figure sitting hunched against a massive tree trunk, arms locked tight about her drawn-up knees. She seemed oblivious of his presence. With a jolt of fear he saw the knife glinting in her hand. He took it from her and she made no move to resist.

"It is not so easy, after all, to kill oneself," she intoned without expression.

"No," he agreed in a curiously tight voice. "Come along, now. It's raining and the ground is very damp. You will take a chill."

She sighed. "It does not matter. I do not think that I can move."

With an exclamation, he lifted her and found her gown already grown sodden. She was passive in his arms and remained so when he left her before the fire in her room while Amy stripped away the wet clothes and enfolded her in thick warm towels, scolding her all the while for laying herself open to a severe inflammation of the lungs.

But she refused to be put to bed and when Theo returned, he found her before the fire, sitting motionless on the rug wrapped in a blanket and staring into the flames.

Amy greeted him with a relief which spilled

over into a scarcely coherent stream of words. "I'm that glad you've come, m'lord. You can see how it is with her . . . not one word has she uttered! It's like she was struck dumb . . . and Cook's good broth sitting there untouched . . ."

Impatiently, Theo signed to her to leave, and when the door had closed, he picked up the steaming bowl and crossed to the fire. Pilar's wet hair clung sleekly to her head and hung, black and shining, against the blanket. The wavering flames emphasized the rigid contours of cheek and jaw.

"Pilar?" He knelt beside her. "What am I to do about you?"

Her state seemed almost trancelike.

"Come," he said gently. "Cook's good boullion will go cold if you do not drink it soon."

There was no sign that she had even heard him.

"Pilar!"

His voice sharpened—and when there was still no response he put down the bowl and, leaning forward, slapped her face—not hard, but with sting enough to make her gasp. Her eyes widened and shifted to stare at him in a little spurt of anger.

"That's better. Now, drink your broth or, by God, I'll hold your nose and tip it down your throat!"

She took it sullenly, and had almost finished it before she began to shake. Theo removed the bowl and took her trembling hands in his, gentle once more.

"Did you really intend to kill yourself?"

"Of course!" Weak tears filled her eyes, spilled over, and fell unheeded. "But I am craven! I lack the resolution for even so simple a task!"

"What an appalling thing to say! How dare you contemplate taking your life!"

"You said it would save you trouble."

"But . . . I didn't mean . . ." Theo straightened up, towering over her. "God in heaven, woman! I say any number of wild, unthinking things when I am in a rage! You do so yourself . . . nobody regards them!"

"Then—you do not mean to have our marriage annulled?"

"No, of course not!"

Was his denial a little too emphatic? She sighed, a strangely desolate sound. "Yet you wish you might, I think." Her shoulders drooped. "Oh, lord—why did you not leave me as I was? Why did you have to marry me?"

"Egad! I remember little enough of the event." Theo confessed ruefully. "I believe I had some overriding notion of settling scores with my esteemed stepmamma!" She turned her head away sharply, but not before he had seen the hurt flare in her eyes. Cursing his clumsy tongue, and to make amends, he added impulsively, "And, of course, I found you eminently desirable . . ."

"Don't!" The cry was wrung from her.

"Deuce take it—now what have I said?"

"At least do me the courtesy not to lie to me, lord!" she cried passionately. "Your desire—if indeed it ever existed—dispersed with the fumes of the wine! There has been little evidence of it since."

"So that's it!" Theo said softly. He put a hand under her chin, drawing her around to face him. He smiled in a way like to melt all resistance. "If that is your humor, the matter is soon remedied!"

"No! That is not what I . . ."

"In point of fact, I had come to a decision this very evening," he continued as if she had not spoken. "We should make a new beginning, you and I. No more fighting . . . no more scenes. What do you say?"

"If that is what you wish," she said slowly, "I would be very pleased not to fight with you."

"Good. Then what better way to set a deal upon our pact. . . ." The blanket was beginning to slip from her shoulders, and Theo pushed it back still further, his eyes lighting with amusement at the sight of the garment it concealed. Of sturdy white cotton, it was high in the neck, tight cuffed, and tied unrelentingly from neck to waist with a series of ribbon bows.

"I'll wager that's Miss Pym's notion of how a nightgown should be!" His fingers moved to loose the ribbons, one by one. "But, no matter. I have overcome worse obstacles in my time!"

"No!" Lost in confusion, she ducked nimbly under his arm and, dragging the blanket around her, sped across the room to stand at last with her back set against him and panic beating helplessly against her ribs. She felt him come up behind her, pluck the blanket from her shoulders, and drop it on the floor. She shivered, but made no further attempt to run.

One hand coiled itself in the damp silken rope of her hair, drawing her close, the other encircled her to dispose of the remaining ribbons and insinuate itself, warmly confident and possessive, against her heart.

"Like the wild fluttering of an imprisoned bird!" he murmured into the bare nape of her neck.

"You are mocking me!" she gasped.

"A little, perhaps." He laughed softly and his lips explored further to where a pulse beat madly.

"Swear that you find my attentions abhorrent and I will let you go."

"You know . . . I cannot! I want . . . I do not want . . ."

"What is it that you want, beautiful Pilar?"

Her reply was scarcely audible. "To be wanted . . . for myself. Not to be taken lightly!"

He turned her to face him. His eyes had grown dark and very brilliant, and she was already lost. He kissed her until the room spun away and she no longer cared why he wanted her!

Pilar woke before it was light. For a moment she wondered why she felt different; could it be the weight across her body which acccounted for the langorous aching in her back and limbs? And then, on a floodtide of remembrance, the weight became an arm, flung carelessly in sleep, fingers curling possessively into the curve of her thigh.

She lay, hardly daring to breathe lest she disturb him—this lord who had taught her the arts of love with such tenderness, such passion, and (she had to acknowledge a still, small voice) such experience, that for a little while she had surrendered herself completely to him. He had been at first surprised by the totality of her response, and then exultant, and finally, his passion all spent, he had fallen asleep quite suddenly with his lips still lingering against her breast.

But she could not sleep so easily; she felt exhilarated, wanting to laugh and cry at the same time. Never had she known it was possible to feel this way. . . . His head grew uncomfortably heavy in the curve of her shoulder and yet she could not bear not to have it there.

She had reached a hand across to smooth the hair
from his brow and without waking, his arms had
tightened, his lips pressing urgently and instinctively into the softness of her breast, almost muf-
fling his murmured endearment.

It was much, much later, when she had counted
the quarters of the little ormolu chiming clock
many times, that sleep finally overtook her.

And now a thin thread of light was beginning to
show along the edges of the curtains, and she
would be confined no longer. Pressing herself flat
into the bed, she eased herself away from Theo.
His fingers tightened momentarily, but though he
grunted his grip relaxed and she slid free. The
despised nightgown lay like a spent ghost, ruthlessly consigned to the floor the previous night. She
slipped it on quickly and crossed to the window,
pulling back the curtain to show a narrow wedge
of pale light.

And there she sat while the pearl gray dawn
turned faintly pink, deepening and flaming finally
into a brief, watery, autumnal brilliance without
depth or permanence. She watched it dry-eyed,
with aching throat, until it faded. Was it always
like this, she wondered bleakly—this unbearable
sense of loss, of desolation, of something beyond
price, forfeited forever?

"Pilar?" Theo's voice made her jump. "You'll
take a chill sitting there," he said persuasively.
"Come back to bed."

She climbed in beside him, subdued—a little awkward. Then he smiled and her heart turned over.

"I thought we had disposed of 'this' last night,"
he murmured, flicking the nightgown with a de-
rogatory finger. His hand slid up under her hair,
caressing her neck, exerting a subtle pressure to

draw her down beside him. She resisted, and a solitary tear splashed onto his shoulder, close to an old dueling scar.

"What's this?" he said quickly. "Tears? From my proud Pilar! I had not thought I had made you so miserable!"

His teasing was unendurable. She shook her head wordlessly and buried her face in his shoulder. Theo held the stiff body until it gradually yielded, plainly puzzled by such odd behavior from this strange, unpredictable creature he had married.

And Pilar, in the bitter-sweet agony of being where she most wanted to be, felt her heart like a stone in her breast; the endearment murmured in that revealing moment of unconsciousness last night still rang like a mockery in her ears. For the name on his lips was not Pilar, but Suzanne!

LORD GILMORE'S BRIDE

8

The Viscount's stepmother arrived on a day of thin winds and sleeting rain—a day well suited to such a visitation, reflected Meecham, as he ushered her ladyship, with her younger daughter, Letty, into the drawing room.

The Dowager seated herself, stiff-backed, upon the least comfortable chair in the room, frowning awfully when the Honorable Letitia Gilmore chose to flop inelegantly upon a yellow velvet sofa. Her voice chilled the atmosphere in spite of a cheerful fire.

"I trust that Lord Gilmore is to be found, Meecham?"

Meecham was aware that word was even now speeding from servant to servant. "If your ladyship will permit, I shall ascertain whether his lordship has returned from his ride."

The door opened to admit Adam Carvray. He came forward swiftly, exchanging an almost imperceptible nod with the departing butler.

"Aunt Gertrude! What an unexpected pleasure—and Letty, too! Theo *will* be surprised. Will you not come a little nearer to the fire? You must be cold after your journey."

"Thank you, no. I do not pander to the body's frailties. Theo has had this room done over, I see!"

94

She cast a jaundiced eye over the pale green walls of the charming octagonal salon, finding little merit in the slim gilded wall mirrors winking between each velvet-draped window, or the gleaming white paintwork and cheerful yellows and golds of the furnishings.

"Such an extraordinary shape!" She dismissed the room with damning finality. "I have always preferred the long drawing room."

Her glance came back to Adam. "I will not beat about the bush. I am here because certain rumors have reached me—rumors which I had fervently hoped might prove groundless." Her thin mouth twitched. "I see from your expression that they are all too true! So. Theo had finally achieved his object—to drag the family name in the dust."

"Oh, come now, ma'am. You do him less than justice!"

"I think not. When a man enters upon a state of matrimony in such a hole and corner fashion, without according his family, much less his friends, the simple courtesy of acquainting them of his intentions—without even a formal notice to the papers—and when that man has been on the verge of becoming betrothed to another, then one can only assume the worst!"

Adam was beginning to feel harried, and cursed Theo for not being on hand to fight his own battles. "Nothing of the kind, ma'am, I do assure you. As to the suddenness, there were reasons. But Pilar is a charming child. You will see, presently."

"But *who is she*, Adam? Pilar! It has a foreign ring!"

"Well . . ."

Letty stroked her velvet muff, her rather shallow, pretty features exuding a deceptive air of innocence. "We heard she was a common gypsy."

"Be quiet, Letitia! *Well*, Adam?"

"Aunt Gertrude . . ."

"Come now, Adam. Don't be mealy-mouthed!"

Unnoticed, Theo had entered the room. Pilar was with him and it was obvious to Adam that their entrance had been carefully planned to create the maximum effect. Pilar wore a polonese of apple green silk he hadn't seen before, looped back in a series of puffs over a hooped petticoat strewn with cream roses. Her head was high and as she tripped imperiously down the length of the room to meet her new-found relations, her fingers rested lightly, yet possessively on her husband's arm.

As she passed Adam, she sent him a mischievous, flicking glance that filled him with foreboding. There had been a subtle shift in her relationship with Theo of late; they no longer rowed, or if they did, it soon ended in laughter . . . and Theo was becoming quite amazingly tolerant! Even when Lady Rackam had called last week in a rainstorm and Pilar had ordered Meecham to bring refreshment, insisting that her ladyship must be 'fair clemmed,' he merely explained with great charm that his wife was still unfamiliar with the English tongue and inclined to pick up phrases from her Yorkshire maid. And though afterward Theo had threatened to wring Pilar's neck, it was plain he had no such intention.

Adam, knowing Theo's facility for engaging a woman's affections, feared that Pilar might be falling victim to his charm . . . and where might that lead?

For the moment, however, it had given her the

necessary composure to face her formidable adversary. She made her curtsy faultlessly.

"As you can see for yourself, ma'am," said Theo smoothly, "there is nothing in the least common about *my wife*." He stressed the last with obvious relish, and the Dowager stiffened.

Letty was staring at her sister-in-law with undisguised curiosity, dwelling with increasing animation upon the dusky complexion, the jet black hair, the bold slanting eyes which dared her to voice her conclusions.

"Why—I believe the rumors were no more than the truth!" she blurted out accusingly.

The Viscount bent upon her a look which made her turn slowly crimson. "I'll make you a present of a little brotherly advice, Letty. You'll be hanging out for a husband yourself any time now, I daresay, and I don't scruple to tell you that you'll never land one unless you learn to bridle that overimpetuous tongue!"

"M-marriage has not m-mellowed you noticeably!" she retorted sulkily.

"Letitia! Be silent! I shall not tell you again. Pilar," the Dowager addressed the new Lady Gilmore rather as though a bad smell hovered under her nose. "Come and sit beside me. I would know more about you."

Pilar spread her skirts and folded her hands unhurriedly in her lap, but just for a moment her eyes lifted to Theo in a kind of query.

"Have no fear, my love," he drawled. "You may speak quite freely. It is all in the family, after all!" With which he turned away to gaze out of the window.

Adam's heart sank.

"You are not English, I think," the cold voice

prodded insistently. "Your speech betrays you and your name is . . . unusual. Spanish, is it not?"

There was a silence.

"My mother was Spanish," Pilar admitted, then lifting her chin, "she was also Romany."

"There! I told you!" cried Letty triumphantly. "A common gypsy!"

Lady Gilmore's breath was drawn in sharply. "One more word, Letitia, and you will leave the room!" She turned a rigid face to Pilar. "Am I to understand that you are actually admitting to your . . . unfortunate connections?"

"There is nothing unfortunate in being Romany," Pilar stated haughtily. "I am proud to be what I am."

"I see." Adam noted that the Dowager's composure had suffered a severe blow. Really! Theo was incorrigible! It was quite obvious that Pilar had been carefully schooled in what she must say. As though to dispel any doubt, Theo turned at that moment from the window with a decided gleam in his eye, already anticipating the next question.

"And your father? Was he also . . . Romany?"

"Oh, no. My father was English. A nobleman."

Lady Gilmore's manner remained frigid. "That is something, I suppose. Were they . . . that is . . . does he own you?"

"Your delicacy of approach does you credit, ma'am," said Theo, amused. "But, no. Pilar don't even know who her father is."

"So!" The Dowager's bosom heaved and the hands groping for her furs trembled visibly. "And this is your chosen Viscountess—the illegitimate offspring of a gypsy and . . . and . . . God knows who! When you could have had Arren's daughter! I do not understand you, Theodore! I am aware

that your morals have always been shockingly lax
. . . it was disgraceful enough that you flaunted
your mistress before the world! But at least Mrs.
Verney's background is unexceptional—and she *is*
received!"

Pilar was finding the conversation difficult to follow, but she was well aware that she was being in-
sulted, and a delicate color stained her cheeks. She
sprang to her feet and Theo came at once to encircle her with his arm.

"Make no mistake, ma'am," he said silkily. "Pilar
will be received. We intend to remove to London
shortly, and there, no door will remain closed to
her if I wish it opened—even in the highest places!"

"Pon rep! Surely you would not attempt to
present her?" Lady Gilmore bristled. "A gypsy
bride! You are indeed mad!"

"I think not. What you have heard this afternoon, is, I need not refine upon it, for your ears—
and yours alone. If one word is leaked abroad . . ."
Here he bent a particularly steely eye upon his half
sister, who shifted sulkily in her chair. ". . . I shall
know from whence it came and I shall not scruple
to deal with the loose tongue accordingly!"

Letty flushed bright red, but Theo had already
lost interest in her. "The world will know what I
choose to tell it—namely that Pilar is Spanish and of
noble extraction. The fiction we have contrived is a
convincing one, and if any guess at the truth, they
will not be so foolish as to voice their doubts."

"Then there is no more to be said. Come Letitia." His stepmother gathered her furs about her
and rose with an air of finality. "I wish you joy of
your mésalliance, Theodore. What your grandparents will make of it all, I do not care to contem-

plate. I am only thankful that your poor papa did not live to witness the family's shame!"

This final censorious thrust failed miserably, for Theo merely put back his head and laughed. "My dear stepmamma, that is pure moonshine and well you know it! My 'poor papa' never gave a fig for anything that didn't interfere with his drinking or his gambling! Adam, dear boy—will you oblige me by ringing for Meecham?" The butler appeared as though on cue. "Ah, Meecham. Her ladyship is leaving. Her carriage . . . ?"

"It is at the door, my lord."

Theo's eyes gleamed with admiration. "Good man. Splendid." He bowed with almost exaggerated courtesy. "Your servant, ma'am. Letty."

When they had gone, Adam said quietly, "Was that wise, Theo?"

"Probably not, my dear—but I have waited twenty years to best that woman! Don't—please —riddle my moment of glory with doubts!" He grinned infectiously and seized Pilar, his hands circling her tiny waist, swinging her off her feet, spinning her dizzily, until she cried Enough—and clung breathlessly to his coat.

"Didn't she carry it off splendidly?"

Adam agreed, but watched them with a troubled smile, again thinking them like a couple of children, intoxicated by their own cleverness. Was he over-reacting in wanting them to have a care?

"If Pilar can hold her own with my insufferable stepmamma, then she can face all comers! I intend to demonstrate my complete confidence in her by taking up Rackam's invitation."

"The New Year Ball at Matcham?" Adam's eyebrows rose a fraction. "You're flying high, Theo. It's usually a pretty grand affair."

"Precisely. It will make a perfect come-out for Pilar! What do you say, my love?" He gave her chin a playful tweak. "Are you ready to make your curtsy to society?"

"If you think I will not disgrace you?" Pilar's words came breathlessly, and she hoped that her heart's beating would pass unheeded. Theo's eyes laughed at her, his indulgent possessiveness enveloped her; at times it made her light-headed, but since that first night she was not fooled! His endearments spilled out with a careless ease borne of much practice. Well, she too could practice guile, coqueting—playing at love, playing his own game and giving to him as much of herself as he might reasonably expect. But her heart's core—that spirit burning deep inside her—*that* she would never give again. It was a resolve that brought her exquisite pain at times—almost she would weaken—and then the name Suzanne would come to lie heavily between them.

Theo's soft laugh now cut across her thoughts. "So pensive? What do you say, Adam? Will my wife disgrace me?"

Adam came and took her hand. His eyes were kind, and something more—compassionate? Almost as though he had read her thoughts.

"Your wife, my dear Theo, will enchant all who meet her," he said quietly.

9

Matcham was ablaze with light on the night of the ball. All had been in a bustle for two days past as the house guests arrived to find the great hall, the salons, and the mirrored ballroom festooned with evergreens. A gentleman in the restrained magnificence of wine velvet and lace moved unhurriedly among the party assembling in the main salon prior to dinner, stopping for a word here and there, and finally being accosted by a late arrival resplendent in a tight cutaway coat and striped breeches tied at the knee with ribbons. He wore a toupee dusted liberally with blue powder, and eyes, piercingly direct, glinted affably from beneath a pair of preposterous eyebrows.

"Francis!" exclaimed Mr. Fox, with a genial lift of those extraordinary brows. "I thought I'd find you here. I've never known you miss a chance to hunt over such fine country as this."

"It depends upon the quarry, my dear Charles," replied Mr. Staveley, with a brief, enigmatic smile. "I do find that in certain circumstances it can become a veritable obsession!"

Mr. Fox thought the smile boded ill for someone, and wondered briefly who had been so unwise as to incur Francis Staveley's displeasure. "Well, I am here for the indoor amusements," he said. "You can always be sure of deep play at Rackam's." He wafted a fan of painted chicken skins on ivory and looked about him. "I perceive that Mrs. Verney is returned from Paris. Do you suppose word of Gilmore's nuptials precipitated her return? There were rumors that they had quarreled violently over the possibility of his marrying Arren's girl. I wonder what she'll make of his final choice, and more particularly, the manner of it?"

Mr. Staveley shrugged an elegant shoulder. "Who can tell, my friend? But it will be amusing to be . . . in at the kill, as it were. Gilmore is to bring the little bride this evening, I'm told." His smile became tinged with malice. "Now, there I *do* own to a certain curiosity! A secret marriage . . . a bride shrouded in mystery? So romantic, don't you think? Some say there are connections with the Spanish nobility, and some are . . . less kind!"

"You should not regard gossip, gentlemen. It can sometimes be quite viciously inaccurate!" Unnoticed, Mrs. Verney had joined them. Her tone was light, almost bantering, but her glance was quick and overbright, and she looked a little white beneath her rouge.

"Suzanne, my dear!" Staveley recovered first, his manner smooth and quite unembarrassed. "May I say that you are truly *ravissante* this evening. There will not be a woman to equal you. Am I not right, Charles?"

Suzanne Verney had indeed surpassed herself. She wore her rich red-gold hair unpowdered, dressed *en herrison* and adorned with curling plumes purchased in Paris at a cost of more than sixty louis a piece. Her gown, too, bespoke Paris, fashioned of pale rose brocade rustling over a hooped lace petticoat.

She knew well enough what was being said, and that it would have been more prudent to have declined the invitation once she knew Theo would be present with his upstart wife. But Suzanne was not noted for her prudence; she was, on the other hand, notorious for her ability to captivate any man who took her fancy . . . and in spite of the violence of their last quarrel, she was not yet ready to relinquish her hold upon Theo. Especially if half she had heard was true!

She therefore set herself to amuse and to captivate, ignoring the speculation of those who whispered behind their fans and who would, no doubt, take a malicious delight in seeing her humbled.

Young Lord Derby claimed her attention and she moved aside to endure politely his shy, rather earnest outpourings. There was a stir near the door of the salon, the crowd parted briefly and then surged forward again—but there had been time enough for Suzanne to have her first glimpse of Lady Gilmore—a slight, vivid, almost regal figure flanked by her three escorts. Whether by accident or design, thought Suzanne in a moment of quite vicious jealousy, she could not have made a more impressive entrance!

White, Theo had stipulated, and white Pilar wore, so that first impressions were of a honey-skinned vision in silver-white gauze and lace, fashioned with exquisite delicacy by Miss Pym.

Tiny brocade slippers, the heels studded with diamonds, peeped from beneath the swaying hem, and she wore a single diamond drop on a necklet, a present from Theo.

Under Fredericks' critical eye, Amy had drawn Pilar's hair—like polished ebony—high into a chignon, from which shining black curls fell in little clusters. To complement the arrangement Fredericks had produced a Spanish comb and delicate lace mantilla. This symplicity of style contrasted quite markedly with some of the more absurd erections bedecked with birds and feathers, adorning the powdered and pomaded heads of the other guests; it emphasized the finely molded contours of her face and gave her an air of aloofness; only when you looked into the sloe-black eyes were you conscious of the fires within.

Francis Staveley stood back from the main body of guests, most of whom were taking elaborate pains to veil their prurient interest in the anticipated confrontation between Gilmore and his mistress. He chose his moment with care, drawing the little bride's glance to himself, watching her start of surprise and widening eyes—with surely just the hint of a plea in their depths? He smiled faintly and inclined his head.

Throughout dinner he watched her, intrigued to see how often those dark eyes sought her husband's across the table, as though seeking reassurance. She ate little, toying daintily—almost nervously—with each course and drinking rather too much.

On the one side, Lord Yarmouth kept up a stream of small talk to which she returned an answer when required to do so, and on the other, Adam Carvray conversed quietly between times. And, further down the table, Hammell leaned forward occasionally to see how she did.

Pilar had known at once who the flame-haired beauty was; it did not need Lord Rackam's drawing Theo aside on their arrival with obvious embarrassment, and Theo's muttered "My God! Suzanne? Here?" or Ham's eagerness to distract her attention to confirm it to her.

It had all been very civilized—in those first moments they had exchanged no more than the most acceptable politenesses, but the air was charged; she could feel the other guests making comparisons; no doubt this Suzanne had attended many such functions in Theo's company; now they were waiting to see how Gilmore's wife would behave, faced with his mistress.

She felt the blood being squeezed out of her body; dinner became a double agony to be endured, but no one, she vowed, would be given cause to find her wanting! She had little idea of what she ate, but the wine slipped down comfortingly and she began to feel that everything might be all right, after all. And later, when dinner was over, Theo stayed close to her, leading her out in the first minute of the ball, introducing her into first one group and then another. . . .

And then, quite suddenly, he wasn't there anymore and Ham was saying solicitously in her ear, "Can I get you a glass of cordial?"

Pilar watched her husband on the far side of the ballroom, his head bent close to an unmistakable red-gold one. There was a disturbing air of intensity about the two figures. She said defiantly, "I would rather have champagne."

Sir Roger had noted the direction of her glance—and of her thoughts. "Now, don't you go getting hold of a lot of foolish notions, *querida*!"

"They are not foolish. She is the one. Those were *her* dresses hanging in the closet at High Tor."

"What if they were?" Sir Roger was silently cursing his friend's indiscretion and wondering where the devil Adam had got to. He was the one to deal with this. "That was months back. What is past is past."

"But it is not past," she said flatly. "Theo is still in love with her. That much is abundantly clear!"

"Oh, lor! Now, look here, Pilar—you musn't go imagining more than needs be! These affairs are quite *de rigeur*, y'know. It don't mean a thing!"

"I rejoice to hear it!" Pilar's eyes were over-bright and there was a stubborn set to her chin. "Though you must not be supposing that I care in the least! Now I will have my champagne, if you please. There is a lackey just passing with a tray." She beckoned imperiously and very reluctantly Sir Roger procured a glass for her.

"I reckon you've had too much already," he said bluntly. "Cordial would be more the thing."

"You are being very unamusing tonight, Ham." She saw Lady Rackam approaching with the man she had met on the downs. Her heart gave a lurch and she seized the glass and began to drink much too quickly, so that the bubbles went up her nose.

"Hey! Steady on, you incorrigible madcap!"

"Ham—who is this man with Lady Rackam?" There was an odd urgent note in her voice.

Sir Roger looked up and groaned. "Francis Staveley! For the Lord's sake, don't start flirting with him! Theo won't like it above half, if you do. He don't care for him overmuch."

Pilar looked in her husband's direction and her chin came up a little higher. "Theo is in no position to dictate *my* behavior!"

Ham greeted Staveley curtly, heard him solicit the privilege of a dance with Pilar, and was aware of a certain something in the air between them. He hesitated, unsure whether to go or stay, and in the end decided to find Adam.

Lady Rackam's presence was presently demanded elsewhere. Staveley watched her go with a quizzical lift of his brow.

"Well, Lady Gilmore!" he drawled. "So we meet ... formally, at last."

"I must thank you, senor, for not betraying that we had met," she said quickly.

"Betray a lady's honor? My dear ma'am, consider how unchivalrous that would make me!" He smiled. "Allow me to get you another glass of champagne. However," he resumed, "I confess my curiosity is only partially allayed. And in the rather ... exceptional circumstances governing our relationship—and if we are to be friends—I am looking to you to gratify it more fully."

Pilar considered him over the rim of her glass. Her back was very straight and there was a tinge of color high on each cheekbone. "I do not understand what it is you are saying, senor. It sounds a little like a threat."

"No—I give you my word!" His eyes held a hint of amusement ... and something else ... something more dangerous. Pilar felt the blood tingling in her veins. This would be an exciting man to know ... but not to trust!

"The whole world talks about Lord Gilmore's marriage," he continued smoothly. "It was, to say the least, sudden! I am agog to learn where Gilmore found such a jewel!"

"Then you are easy to gratify, for there is no mystery. I was in the North of England, staying with friends near Theo's shooting lodge. We met and fell in love. You see how simple a story it is?"

The well-rehearsed lies had tumbled out with

ease, but she could wish she had not sounded so breathless.

"You disappoint me, my lady! I confess I had hoped for some great saga of romance and intrigue. You have only to add that the union was blessed with full parental consent and I shall be well and truly cast down."

"Then I can save you that much, at least, senor," Pilar blurted out. "There were no parents to give consent, for my mother died soon after our arrival in England, and having no reason to return to Spain, I remained in Yorkshire."

"I am sorry. And your father?"

The question echoed in her head, but the answer came quite positively, after only a moment's pause. "Dead many years."

"Ah!" said Mr. Staveley softly. "That is tragic. But, you see, I was right, after all. Already the story becomes more intriguing. A young girl—a stranger to our shores—is tragically orphaned and when all seems lost, she meets and falls in love with a handsome young English lord. Is this not the very stuff of romance?"

Pilar felt a giggle bubbling up; she was beginning to have a delicious sensation of floating. How fortunate that she should meet this Mr. Staveley who was so charming and amusing.

"You make it appear so, indeed!"

He looked at the diamond pendant for a moment in pensive silence. "And that day we met," he added casually, "you cannot deny that you were at great pains to be secretive."

She pouted. "Ah, but then, I was breaking the rules, you see. I had ridden too far . . . and had no groom. . . . My husband was . . . would be angry, if he knew. I am still not quite used to your English ways," she finished, feeling flustered.

"Of course. And yet," he said with gentle emphasis, "you surprise me again, for I had always understood that the Spanish reared their young ladies with the utmost strictness!" He watched her confusion with interest and then, as the music began to swell, said smoothly, "I believe this is the dance you promised me, Lady Gilmore?"

Sir Roger was turned aside several times in his efforts to find Adam. He finally ran him to earth in one of the smaller salons, where a group including the Earl of Derby, Sir Charles Bunbury of the Jockey Club, Mr. Fox, and Lord Grosvenor were deep in horse talk.

"Over here, Ham!" called Mr. Fox. "As a racing man, this should interest you. Young Derby here's so puffed up with the success of that new race of his . . ."

"The Oak's, d'you mean?"

"That's the one. Well, it's proved so popular that he and Bunbury are to initiate another one-and-a-half-miler, for colts as well as fillies this time."

"Sounds a capital notion. How will you name this one, my lord? After another of your houses? The Knowsley Stakes, perhaps?"

This began a spate of suggestions, not destined to be taken seriously, and finally the Earl said diffidently, "We had thought to name it The Derby and to run it in early May."

The discussion continued in a lively manner and it was some time before Sir Roger recalled the reason for his seeking Adam out.

"Look here, You'd best come and keep an eye on young Pilar. Silly chit's getting a sight too friendly with Francis Staveley—*and* she's dipping into the champagne. 'Tis a combination I mislike!"

Adam frowned. "Is Theo not with her?"

"No, he ain't!" Ham snorted. " 'The Verney' has got her claws into him, and Theo, curse him, has eyes for no one else. I only hope he don't live to regret it."

Regrets Theo was certainly having; his friends would have been dismayed to learn their extent. Faced with Suzanne suddenly like this he was totally unprepared; all the old desire came rushing in. She was all and more than he had remembered, a beautiful, tantalizing woman drawing him inexorably to her side. His obligations to Pilar faded into oblivion as the blood beat in his veins.

He could not have told what they spoke of in those first moments together; it was enough to have her near, her smile warm but tinged with sadness as she rested slim white fingers lightly against the rich purple of his sleeve.

"Why did you do it, my dear?" she queried, and there was the hint of a break in her voice. "Did our quarrel seem so final? Surely you knew I must have come around in time!"

"You gave me little cause for hope."

"Oh my dear! You make me feel responsible for the tragedy of this headlong rush into marriage. Lady Eustacie I must have accepted as inevitable, but to take this unknown child! Was it to spite me?"

Theo's face took on the closed look of arrogance she knew so well.

"We will not discuss my marriage, if you please. Not now—not ever."

Suzanne could have bitten on her tongue. Hastening to retrieve her error, she laughed lightly.

"Indeed, no, my love—I could not bear to let another quarrel come between us. I have been utterly wretched away from you!"

"We cannot talk here," Theo said reluctantly. "I must find Pilar."

"By all means, my love—if you deem it necessary. But I believe she has just taken the floor with Francis Staveley."

The gentle malice was lost on Theo. His eyes found the figure of his wife—saw her laughing up into Staveley's eyes. The sight filled him with quite unwarranted annoyance. Suzanne seized her opportunity.

"Perhaps, since there is little you can do for the present, you will bear me company a while longer—I promise to be most circumspect. Shall we go into the salon where it is a little quieter?"

It was considerably later when Adam found them. He cut abruptly into what Theo was saying with less than his customary good manners—excusing himself briefly to Suzanne and drawing Theo out of earshot.

"For God's sake, man! Are you deaf and blind? Or simply uncaring that all your work is being undone. Can you not hear the commotion in the ballroom?"

Theo became aware of the music's familiar throbbing insistence, but the full horror only dawned on him as they arrived on the scene. The center of the ballroom floor had been cleared and was ringed by a solid wall of people blocking the view. But he knew what he would find even as he pushed his way to the front. There was a glazed look in his eyes. Adam followed, laying an urgent, restraining hand on his arm. "Gently, coz! Make a scene, and the whole world will know of it—and ridicule you thereafter!"

He thought Theo was beyond hearing, but on the edge of the floor he halted beside a wretched Sir Roger, watching his wife whirling around the floor with the abandon of that first night in the gypsy camp.

"How?" he demanded savagely of Ham. "What the devil were you about to let her make such an exhibition of herself?"

Anger flared briefly in the good-humored face. "I was attempting to fill your shoes, my lord—a task that sits ill with me as you have now learned to your cost."

Theo flushed darkly, but before he could say more, the music ended.

Pilar, sunk in a deep curtsy, was wondering how she would ever rise to her feet again. She felt decidedly odd; her head swam giddily; her ears rang with disembodied cheers, a cruelly derisive sound.

And then the decision was taken from her; arms like iron bands lifted her and Theo's voice was in her ear—soft, but more angry than she had ever heard it.

"Stand up straight and walk out with your head high, or, by God, I'll drop you back on the floor and wash my hands of you."

With his arm taking most of her weight, she negotiated a path between the press of people undulating in the trembling candlelight; it parted in shocked waves of silence to let them pass and closed in again behind them with a subdued, buzz of whispering.

The portly figure of their host swam into view—of Lady Rackam there was no sign. Theo was speaking again, his apologies curt. ". . . Lady Gilmore . . . not quite herself . . . with your permission I will get her home."

The reassurances and commiserations came smoothly enough ". . . the heat in the room . . . Lady Rackam is herself a trifle indisposed . . . and asks me to offer her excuses."

Pilar was dimly aware that something was expected of her, but felt quite unable to curtsy. She extended a gracious hand and smiled with foolish brilliance.

"Lord Rackam—*gracias*. Please to convey to your wife my thanks a-and good w-wishes for her speedy recovery."

And Rackam, looking for sarcasm, found only that wide-eyed, innocent smile.

As they left, the whispering in the ballroom exploded into a babel of sound. Amusement and outrage mingled with critical conjecture. Suzanne Verney didn't hear Mr. Staveley come up behind her; his voice in her ear was gently sardonic.

"I wonder how Lady Gilmore was persuaded to perform in such a way? A curiously fortuitous incident from your viewpoint, my dear Suzanne—if indeed luck had any part in it!"

Mrs. Verney turned slowly, a slight frown creasing the flawless brow, blue eyes questioning.

"Of course," he continued blandly, "I might have been mistaken in supposing that I caught a glimpse of you earlier, conversing with the orchestra leader."

"I do not converse with musicians." Mrs. Verney was coldly positive.

"No? And yet I could have sworn . . . your hair, my dear . . . such a glorious color and so distinctive!" He watched the blood creep under her skin and smiled. "Have no fear. It is not my intention to spoil sport. You see, I too have an interest—mayhap we can help one another!"

A hoar frost glittered in the hedgerows. The air, so sharp and clear, brought the black, star-strewn sky very close, polishing it to a shining clarity.

The first gasp of icy air made Pilar sway giddily, but she was hustled ruthlessly into the waiting coach. The silence grew oppressive—she attempted at first to relieve it with a defiant burst of singing, but an urgent prod from Ham silenced her; also the jolting along the hard rutted road was beginning to make her feel queasy.

Any hope that retribution might be deferred until morning was dashed as soon as Pilar had negotiated the staircase with the unobtrusive assistance of Adam and Sir Roger. Theo strode ahead and flung open the drawing room door.

"In here!"

Adam said quietly, "If you'll take my advice for once, Theo, you'll sleep on it. Recriminations are useless. Pilar is in no case to . . ." He was cut short abruptly.

"Thank you, coz. I believe I am the best judge of my wife's condition. We will have it out now, if you please!" Theo's fingers closed on Pilar's wrist and she was plucked from the safe custody of her two would-be protectors and propelled willy-nilly across the threshold.

Sir Roger protested angrily.

"Alone," Theo added, closing the doors against further argument.

Pilar stumbled across the vast expanse of gold carpet, wishing it wouldn't tilt so under her, and huddled into a sofa before the fire, which blazed but left her cold. The last of her elation had drained away. Her head began a slow pounding and she wished very much to be dead.

She felt rather than saw Theo come to stand over her. "Well, Pilar? Are you satisfied?"

Her head moved in weary negation.

"I must take it, I suppose, that your protestations of the past weeks that you wished to be a credit to me were mere play acting?"

"No!"

"No? How else, then, am I to interpret this evening's behavior?"

"It must have been the champagne," she muttered miserably.

"Oh, I see!" The soft cutting irony roused her.

"No, you do not see! And you are making altogether too much fuss! My dancing was very much admired. Did you not hear the applause?"

"Oh yes! But applause? I would rather term it the kind of ovation traditionally reserved for a very different kind of entertainment—one not usually to be found in a gentleman's ballroom!"

Pilar sprang up. "*Odioso!* You are a wicked liar! It was not like that!"

"Was it not? Then take a good look at yourself, *Lady Gilmore!*" His fingers bit into her shoulders, lifting her, swinging her around to face one of the long wall mirrors set between the windows. Even the kindly candlelight could not soften her high flush or disguise the trailing mantilla, the sad wisps of hair clinging lankly to the nape of her neck. "*My wife!*" he taunted with a bitter laugh. "My God! You are a disgrace!"

Angry tears blurred her eyes. "And if I am, who is the most at fault? Were you at my side to support me through the ordeal of my first public appearance?"

She was right, but the realization only infuriated him the more. "You had been well schooled—you had no need of me. Besides, Sir Roger and Adam were there to look after you, though heaven knows they made poor work of it!"

Pilar wrenched herself free. "Do not blame your friends, do you hear me? I love them both dearly—and if I am sorry at all it is that I have failed *them*! As you failed me!"

"And it was to spite me, I suppose, that you engaged the attentions of the first smooth-tongued philanderer to make a play for you?"

"Ha!" She laughed wildly. "If I did not know better, I might suppose you to be jealous! Mr. Staveley was most kind to me. . . ."

"Then he had a reason. Staveley never does anything without a reason. He is ruled by ambition and vanity."

"You do not like him, that much is plain." Pilar flung the words scornfully. "But are you so blameless that you can talk of philandering? *She* had only to beckon, and in that moment I ceased to exist for you!"

"That will do, Pilar!"

"No! It will not do!" She was plunging recklessly now, but anger and a deep sense of injustice carried her on. "I know that she is your woman since a long time! And from what I saw tonight it is apparent to me that she is to continue so. I wonder that you did not choose to make *her* your wife."

"So do I, by God! At least Suzanne knows how to conduct herself!"

His face was taut, his eyes narrowed to glittering

slits. Pilar scrubbed at a tear that rolled traitorously down her cheek.

"Ah, that is unjust! And it is untrue. I know very well how to behave! If I blundered, it was because of inexperience—and because I was so enraged to see you flaunting yourself with that . . . *puta*!"

His slap made her gasp. "Don't ever let me hear a word like that on your lips again. Do you understand me?"

She nursed her stinging cheek and glared back resentfully. "It is what she is!" she muttered. "Call it what you will!"

"And you, my dear, are a jealous, ill-tempered little half-breed gypsy brat, so don't start giving yourself airs!"

She was silenced at last. Feeling sick and with her head pounding miserably, she turned and fumbled her way back to the sofa.

"I cannot help it if you prefer her instead of me!" The words were plainly choking her. She drew a breath as though there was not air enough in the room to ease her lungs. "We do not have a love match, after all. You may do as you please. *But do not call me names*, do you hear? Whatever I am, is what you have made of me! And any mistakes were as much yours as mine. . . ."

Theo heard the break in her voice. It had the oddest affect on him—for he experienced an overwhelming urge to gather the hunched, forlorn figure into his arms; to comfort her; to confess that the whole of the blame was his. But he hardened his heart.

"You are right," he said stiffly. "I probably expected too much. Go along to bed now. You're going to have a terrible head in the morning."

"Will you send me away?" He could almost hear the held breath.

"No. But plainly the removal to London must wait. There will be talk. Better for you to stay here for the present—until the gossip dies down and you are better versed in your role." He avoided her eyes as he spoke. "Perhaps I can find that female companion for you. Adam said you should have had one from the first. He is usually right, curse him!"

"Oh, but I don't want . . ." Pilar began, and stopped. "Oh, well—it doesn't matter." Her legs felt woolly when she stood, but there was a desperate pride in the poker-straight back as she walked past him to the door. "If I humiliated you tonight, I am sorry." She drew a sighing breath. "But then, you also humiliated me."

She did not wait for an answer.

10

Pilar was in her small back parlor when Sir Roger came to take his leave. Having passed a sleepless night, she had been roused by Amy from a fitful, head-throbbing doze with the news that Lord Gilmore had driven off at first light, like all the devils were on his tail. Amy's eyes were big with unasked questions, but her mistress was in no mood to gratify her curiosity and cut her short.

Sir Roger twisted his hat uncomfortably, aware that he had failed Pilar. The interview was painful to both of them.

"Can't stay with Theo gone," he said. "Not at all the thing. Dashed bad business . . . all my fault."

"No! You must not say so!" She seized his hand in both of hers. "I shall miss you, dear Sir Ham, but we shall meet very soon. Yes?"

"Of course. Not a doubt of it," he said gruffly. "Theo will come to his senses soon enough. You'll see. Not that he deserves . . . but then . . ."

Adam said much the same thing. He found her standing at the window—and thought how terribly ill and drawn she looked in the merciless rays of the winter sunlight dancing through the small leaded panes. There was an unbearable, untouchable dignity about her—like that of a slim, composed madonna. It came to him suddenly how much she had grown into her role without their even noticing.

But he knew that composure for the brittle thing it was—a word wrong and it would crumble, and she would hate that. He kept to practicalities.

"I shall be staying with Colonel Tracy at Witherington. Meecham will know how to reach me if you need me—but in any case, I shall ride over each day to see how you do."

"Thank you." She plucked nervously at the green plush curtains. "Will Theo come back, do you suppose?"

"Good Lord—yes, of course he will! Before long he will be missing you like the very devil!"

He saw her hand tighten until the knuckles showed white. "He should have left me a gypsy. I was not happy then, either, but at least I knew my appointed station in life." Her voice sharpened with bitterness. "Now I no longer know what I am!"

Adam was surprised by the wave of anger that swept him; it led him to cross the room and take hold of her with unaccustomed force. "You are Lady Gilmore—a very beautiful and enchanting young lady, worthy to grace any man's home—and don't you ever forget it!" He gave her a little shake. "One day soon the world too will know it!"

"Oh, Adam!" Pilar kissed him impulsively. "I should have married you, who are so kind! You would never be unreasonable or expect the impossible of me!"

"Or fight with you—or bring that telltale sparkle to your eye," Adam finished mockingly, so that she should not know how her words had affected him. "No, my dear, I should make a very dull husband."

Pilar insisted on walking with him to the door, standing to wave him from sight, heedless of the

cold. Then she ran up the staircase, feeling
Meecham's eyes on her, and in the privacy of her
bedchamber broke down in a passion of weeping.

Amy watched in dismay, stricken to silence by
the heart-shaking storm of mingled grief and temper. This was how she had been in the early days,
tearing off the pretty dress, pulling on her riding
habit, berating Amy violently when she did not do
up the buttons "*instantamente!*"

"In a terrible taking she was!" Amy confided to
Cook later, down in the servant's hall. "Something
dreadful must've happened last night!"

"Aye, well—blood will out!" came the cryptic
reply.

"That's unfair, and downright ungrateful! She's
been right kindly to you—done your screws a
power of good with her potions. No—if you ask
me, 'tis my belief they quarreled bad!" Amy
warmed to her theme, stirred to the very depths of
her romantic soul by the drama of it all.

"And now his lordship's gone off and left her
and she's mortal grieved—heartbroken at his going!"

Her mistress, meantime, was riding dangerously,
defiantly fast over the hard-packed ground with
her hair streaming free, hurling her rage into the
mounting wind, which snatched it and tossed it,
echoing, into the low, racing clouds. For answer
the rain came, laced with hail, slashing and beating
into her upturned face already streaked with tears.

She had tried! *En nombre de Dios*, she had tried!
All those lessons . . . the abominable stays . . . the
hours and days and weeks of discomfort and obli-
gation! And all had been for nothing!

The mare whinnied in terror as the hail suddenly
became a battering, deafening onslaught. Pilar

clung to the mare's neck, sobbing out an incoherent stream of comfort—as much for herself as for May-fly.

The storm, though violent, was mercifully brief; it left behind a trail of torn branches—and in Pilar a hopeless void.

For the rest of the day she was subdued. When Meecham announced a visitor, she was sitting disconsolately before the fire in the salon, brooding over her marriage lines. She quickly folded the paper and pushed it back into the little gold box as Mr. Staveley came forward.

"Lady Gilmore. Forgive me. I am intruding!"

She said hurriedly, "Not at all, senor. My husband has . . . been called away, but you are most welcome."

"Thank you, ma'am. Nevertheless, I will not stay above a moment." All trace of tears had faded, but there was a look of strain which did not escape him any more than did the painful wave of color which came and went. "I came merely to assure myself that you had recovered from your . . . indisposition of last evening."

Pilar stared up at him; it was inconceivable that he should not know the truth! All must have been aware of her shame. He met her questioning stare without embarrassment.

"You do not have to be kind, senor. I made myself a spectacle, did I not? I am ashamed."

"Then you must not be," said Mr. Staveley. "May I sit for a moment?"

"Oh, please! I am remiss!"

She indicated a chair opposite, but he came instead to sit beside her on the sofa. She was very much aware of his closeness and sat with her hands

clasped around the little box, her eyes veiled by
their long lashes.

Mr. Staveley thought he had never seen a head so
proud, a neck curving so exquisitely from gently
drooping shoulders—and felt a momentary pity.

"Lady Gilmore—will you permit a cynical ob-
server of our fickle society to advise one who is not
yet, I think, quite at ease in that society?"

She looked up guiltily to meet his rather intent
gaze.

"I have no wish to probe, ma'am. . . ."

"But perhaps you wonder . . . there must have
been talk . . . last night . . ."

"I take no account of talk," he said, "and no
more should you. As to last night, my advise is—
forget it. Others will, soon enough. And never
apologize for your mistakes."

Mr. Staveley stood up to leave—and as she too
rose, his eye lighted on what she held.

"That is a most attractive box—a snuff box,
surely?"

"I do not know. It was my mother's. I always
supposed my father gave it to her."

"May I see?"

Pilar surrendered it with reluctance and he subjected it to a minute scrutiny. "A beautiful piece,"
he murmured. "Unique in its way. The box is
French—by Ducrolly—and these miniatures are
signed. Rare! Exquisite! I doubt there being another quite like it! Do you mind?" Before she
knew it, he had opened it, and her piece of paper
fell out. She retrieved it with obvious embarrassment and he begged forgiveness for his clumsiness,
but retained his hold on the snuff box.

"As you will have gathered, such objects are

something of a passion with me," he confessed. "I cannot persuade you to part with it, I suppose?"

"Oh no!"

"Of course," he said suavely. "A family keepsake! I cannot remember if you mentioned—was your father French?"

"But no—he was English!" Why had she told him—a near stranger? Only Mr. Staveley did not seem at all a stranger. Perhaps she could ask him to say nothing. "Please," she began, found he was watching her troubled face intently, and lost her courage. "It is nothing. May I have my box back, please?"

He put it into her hand, his eyes holding hers. "Lady Gilmore—I would like to think we were friends? If there is ever any way I can be of service, please do not fail to call on me."

Mr. Staveley's visit served to emphasize her isolation. With the exception of Adam, no one came near; no cards were left. And since many of the people at Lord Rackam's ball were local, she must assume that Theo was proved right—she had plainly been judged and found wanting!

She took to spending a lot of time in the small back parlor, sketching—an accomplishment for which she had developed a talent and which gave her a certain pleasure.

She didn't see the carriage arrive in a flurry of snow or the tiny lady who descended in a quantity of purple velvet and slipping sables, her extraordinary red frizzed wig crowned by an enormous brimmed hat nodding with plumes.

Meecham was at the door to receive her. "Good day, Lady Penridding. May I say how pleasant it is to see your ladyship? And looking so well."

The Countess's eyes twinkled. "Thank you,

Meecham—I have braved the inclement weather, as
you see, in order to visit my grandson and make
the acquaintance of his wife."

Meecham's face betrayed nothing. "I very much
regret, ma'am, Lord Gilmore is not home at
present."

"Confound the boy! And Lady Gilmore?" His
hesitation was not lost upon her. "Well, man? Is
she here, or is she not?"

"Her ladyship is, I believe, in the back parlor,
ma'am. I will take you up."

"Don't put yourself about—I'll announce myself.
I have a fancy to take her unawares." She set one
neat booted foot on the stair, which brought her
bright, birdlike gaze level with his. "What is she
like, Meecham?"

"My lady?"

"Come! Don't dissemble, man! We've known
one another too long to stand on ceremony. Is the
child a scheming minx, as my late son's widow
would have me believe, or is she not?"

"That you must judge for yourself, my lady,"
said Meecham gravely. "I can only tell you that
Lady Gilmore is very well thought of below
stairs."

"Humph!" said the Countess of Penridding.

Pilar was in no mood to receive company. She had
awoken with a fit of the dismals, snapping Amy's
head off when she had attempted to be cheerful.

When the door opened, she was drooping over
the spinet picking out a tune with one finger. Her
astonishment was almost ludicrous on beholding the
sharp-featured apparition standing before her.

"*En nombre de Dios!*" she exclaimed, frowning.
"How has Meecham let you up the stairs? If you
are the one Theo has sent to be some kind of du-

enna, then you may leave at once, for I do not wish to have you!"

The Countess cast her sables onto a nearby chair and crossed to the fire. "Do I look like a duenna?" she quizzed, holding out thin, clawlike fingers to the flames and studying this latest addition to her family. A gypsy? Undoubtedly. But common? Surely not! There was an undoubted fieriness of spirit—a willful pout to that full red mouth, which owed nothing to paint. But there was pride, too, in the tilt of her chin, the way she carried herself. Lady Penridding found herself consumed with curiosity about her parentage.

Pilar was beginning to feel uncomfortable under the scrutiny of this strange-looking woman who had come unannounced. Perhaps she was mad! It would be wise, then, to humor her.

She said warily, "I do not know how a duenna should look, but we have not met, for I would not easily forget you . . . and I cannot think why else you are here. Will you not sit down and tell me. . . ? And perhaps take some tea?"

The Countess laughed, a sharp, tinkling sound. "Very well done, child! Come—let us have an end to teasing. I will set your mind at ease. Has Theo never spoken to you of his grandparents?"

His grandmother. But of course! What was it Ham had said of her? "Lady Penridding . . . a great character! Ugly as sin, don't you know, but a heart of gold . . . and she dotes on Theo, though you'd not guess at it . . . tongue like a rapier's thrust!" *Madre!* Whatever must she think!

"I am sorry . . . I did not know you . . ."

"Bless you, child! How could you know me when that wretched boy hides you away down here instead of bringing you on a visit? Where is Theo, by the way? Newmarket, I'll warrant—or somewhere equally unsavory!"

The air of deep unhappiness had not escaped her, but she gave no sign that she had noticed. "No matter. We shall become acquainted better without him."

It suddenly seemed important to Pilar that she should not be deceived. "You must wonder at Theo's choice . . ." she began resolutely.

"I gave over wondering at that boy's quirks a long time back." Lady Penridding, as always, was prepared to follow her instincts. "It would seem to me that he could scarcely have done better."

"But perhaps you do not understand . . ." For the first time she found the confession difficult. ". . . I am gypsy."

"Only half-gypsy, surely!" A quantity of bracelets jangled on brittle wrists. "Gertrude almost always gets her facts wrong. But half or whole, 'tis of little consequence."

"You don't mind?" Pilar had left the spinet and drawn closer to this odd little lady who had now cast her hat after the furs, revealing the red hair in its full glory, and settled herself into a capacious armchair which left her legs dangling above the ground.

"Mind, child—why should I mind?" Her eyes twinkled wickedly. "If the family can tolerate an old scarecrow like me, they can tolerate you. Shouldn't wonder if an infusion of good, vigorous gypsy blood don't do the Gilmores a power of good!"

Pilar smiled uncertainly. "Theo is already regretting it, I think. I cannot be what he wants, you see." She related the whole of her disgrace.

Lady Penridding snorted. "Trust Theo to make a botch of it! God love us! The boy hasn't got the sense he was born with! Can he not see what is under his nose? You have great individuality m'dear—it should be developed, not stifled." She flung a hand in the direction of the bellrope and set her bracelets jangling again. "Ring for that tea, Pilar. We must decide what is to be done. Oh, what a good thing I came! Will you put yourself in my hands, child?"

Pilar felt a tiny bubble of excitement. "To what purpose, madam?"

"Why—to complete your education, of course!"

Theo found Town disappointingly thin of people. He made a determined attempt to expunge all memory of his disastrous marriage from his mind, resorted to gambling, and soon his pockets were the lighter by two thousand pounds.

Suzanne Verney, at her most charming, set herself to comfort, cajole, and make herself once more indispensable—and might have succeeded had not Theo come face to face with Ham in White's. Ham cut him dead.

Three bottles of port later, self-contempt drowned in self-pity, he stumbled back to his house in Arlington Street and was put to bed by Fredericks. There, his dreams were persistently invaded by a whirling gypsy figure, black hair flying.

A visit to Newmarket recouped his two thousand pounds but failed to rid him of an unendurable longing. He admitted defeat and arrived at Ashenden in a blinding squall of snow to be informed that her ladyship was gone away.

The Viscount stripped off his gloves and threw

them on the table. "Gone away? What do you mean, 'gone away'? Dammit, where would she go? She don't know anyone!"

Meecham took his hat and driving coat and passed them to a waiting lackey. He coughed delicately. "I should perhaps add, my lord, that Lady Penridding arrived for a visit in your lordship's absence."

"My grandmother! Egad! They clashed, of course! Still, Pilar had no call to run away!" Theo had a sudden, frightening memory of a rain-soaked night and a passionate cry: "I will kill myself!"

But this was different . . . She had no reason . . . "Wasn't Mr. Carvray here?" he snapped. "He could have reassured Lady Gilmore that she had nothing to fear from my grandmother's tongue."

"Mr. Carvray has been a daily visitor, my lord." Meecham's expression was bland. "But indeed, the two ladies appeared to deal quite amicably together. When Lady Penridding departed, Lady Gilmore accompanied her."

"The devil she did! Where did they go?"

"I believe their ultimate destination was Paris, my lord."

The lackey found hat and coat snatched from his arms as the Viscount went storming off toward the stables, shouting for his horse.

At Witherington, Colonel Tracy wasn't sure where Adam might be located. He suggested Lord Gilmore might try some of his more outlying tenant farms. Carvray had spoken of doing a tour of inspection.

After several abortive sorties, Theo finally ran his cousin to earth three miles away, taking tea with the Parkers in their cozy chintz-hung parlor, looking remarkably snug and complacent before a big log fire. His arrival set the good wife in a fluster, wondering if his lordship would be pleased to come to the fire and take a dish of tea—or perhaps Mr. Parker could offer him something stronger to keep out the cold?

Theo declined abruptly, cast a fulminating glance at Adam, and spoke cryptically of urgent business. Adam guessed from the restive fury in Theo's face what that business must be. With a sigh of regret for the blazing fire and the scarcely diminished pile of home-baked scones, he rose to take his leave.

Theo fumed with ill-concealed impatience while the horses were brought and matters of little importance given a final airing.

The moment they were out of earshot, he demanded brusquely, "What is this damned nonsense about Paris?"

"Ah! Meecham told you, did he? Well, there's no mystery, my boy. Lady Penridding decided that Pilar would benefit from a few weeks in her company and where better to complete Pilar's education than Paris. She left a message, should you return, that you would be welcome to join them." Adam paused significantly. "Shall you go?"

But Theo was filled with a wild, unreasoning sense of outrage. He had driven like the very devil from Town, expecting to find his wife suitably chastened, longing for his return, and ready to throw herself into his arms. He had resolved, in his imaginings, to accept her overtures with magnanimity—to cosset her, indulge her. And what did he find? Not only was she not missing him—she had gone off without a thought for him. No message—not a word!

"No!" he declared angrily. "I'll be damned if I go trailing on their heels!"

His face was more expressive than he knew. Adam, watching him vanish into the swirling snow, looked at first thoughtful and then began to smile.

11

On a day when a sprightly breeze teased the blossoms from the trees in London parks and chivvied it into fragrant, snowy drifts, a traveling coach piled high with bandboxes and portmanteaus clattered into Berkeley Square and drew up before Penridding House. It was followed by another, smaller carriage, equally laden.

A slim young exquisite stepped down and turned to offer his hand to a tiny, grotesque lady, defiantly past middle age, in a tall hat bristling with feathers, very much *à la mode Parisienne*—and following on her heels, a vision in palest green velvet.

The news reached Theo that same evening during a card party at Mrs. Verney's pretty little house on the fringe of the fashionable part of town. Suzanne had married the dull, but highly respectable Mr. Verney when he was in his dotage. He had survived the union for scarcely a twelvemonth, leaving his widow sufficiently endowed to enable her to do the house over entirely to her liking; with the addition of a few choice pieces of French furniture and new rose brocade hangings, her salon was very soon the venue for the smart and the tonish—and none was a more frequent visitor than Lord Gilmore.

Mrs. Verney was unsettled by the news of Pilar's

return. In her absence she had largely retrieved the position so foolishly jeopardized by that stupid quarrel. This time she would have to be much cleverer. This marriage, a mésalliance if she ever saw one, could not—must not—be allowed to flourish. Already it was on shaky ground, thanks to that disastrous evening at Rackam's and given time, the Spanish gypsy chit would surely dig her own pit and fall into it—if necessary, she could be helped on her way yet again.

And then? Well, divorce was not unheard of—and what more natural than that Theo should turn to the woman who had stood so uncomplainingly beside him?

Theo had been losing steadily all evening and wasn't in the best of humors when he became aware of the talk.

". . . Harry was on his way to the Club . . . saw the Penridding coach arrive . . . groaning under a mountain of baggage . . . lackeys running back and forth . . . quite a spectacle, by all accounts . . . and young Hammell directing operations . . . the ladies in prime form!"

Theo pushed his chair back abruptly—and all eyes turned on him in varying degrees of expectation.

The official story that Lady Penridding's health had been the reason for her abrupt departure for France, taking Pilar as companion and prop, had been received with a cynicism bordering on open disbelief.

Dick Sheridan's blue eyes twinkled. "Shouldn't have thought to see you here at all this evening, Gilmore—with that deuced pretty little wife of yours restored to your bosom!"

There was general laughter.

Theo stiffened. Suzanne was at his side, the pressure of her hand on his arm warning him to have a care. She laughed lightly, "Well, at all events, it seems Lady Gilmore has not lacked for company in her travels!"

"Saw Staveley last week," said a man called Grant. "Just come back from France . . . said he had the pleasure of escorting the two ladies to the theater!" He wilted slightly under Theo's glare. "In-cidently, my lord, S-Staveley reckoned your w-wife was causing no small stir in Paris!"

The intelligence did nothing to diminish Theo's growing indignation. He would not be made a fool of!

"You'll not be going to Epsom now, of course," Fox pressed him waggishly. "Better things to do, I'll warrant!"

Theo stood up and made his way to the buffet laid out on side tables. He put up his glass and unhurriedly selected a goose liver patty. "What? Miss Derby's new classic chase?" he drawled. "My dear Charles—I would not miss it for the world!"

There was a brief note from his grandmother awaiting him when he returned to Arlington Street the following morning. Fredericks presented it in a reproachful silence. The note requested Theo's attendance at his earliest convenience.

"When did this come?"

"At about four o'clock yesterday afternoon, my lord. I took the liberty of informing her ladyship that you were from home, and we were not sure when to look for your return."

"Highly enterprising of you," said the Viscount harshly. "No doubt you consider I should present myself in Berkeley Square without further delay?"

"Oh hardly so early, my lord." Fredericks eyed

his master's dress with veiled disapproval. "I would suggest the new blue coat with the mother-of-pearl buttons—er, black small clothes and perhaps the new striped waistcoat?"

Theo strode toward his dressing room, stripping off his cravat as he went.

"Very nice—but you'll oblige me by laying out my riding clothes, and quickly."

"My lord?"

"Come, man—you've never forgotten what day it is? The fourth of May. I have a prior engagement at Epsom."

"Horse racing, my lord?" Fredericks queried faintly.

"Precisely."

"But . . . what of Lady Penridding?" He very much wanted to add "your wife," but even he would not dare so far!

His lord and master was not entirely stupid, however. There was a gleam in his eye. "You may tell *anyone* who inquires further for me, whatever you consider appropriate. You will know how to turn 'em up sweet!"

It was two days later, in the afternoon, that Theo finally arrived in Berkeley Square. He was shown up to the sunny drawing room where he found his grandmother sitting alone, straight-backed in her chair, her frizzed hair flaming incongruously against pink brocade cushions.

Bird-bright eyes looked him over, the continuing silence reproaching him for the unwarranted casualness of his dress—his dust-laden boots in particular.

"Well, Theodore," she said at last. "I suppose we must be grateful that you have seen fit to honor us with a visit, but having waited so long, I believe we might have contained our impatience a little longer in order that you might dress."

Theo flushed at the reproof, but bent nevertheless to kiss the highly rouged cheek. "Grandmother. I hope I find you well?"

"Tolerably so, I thank you, child," said her ladyship dryly. "Your concern for my health would be more flattering, however, had it been less tardily expressed."

"Your continuing good health must always be my concern, ma'am," Theo said stiffly. "I came as soon as I could."

She looked at him until he flung away to stare down into the fire, which burned though the day was warm. A footman came in bearing Madeira. He set the tray down on a table near the window. Theo waved him away impatiently and poured his own.

"Where is Collinson?" he asked abruptly. "A very odd man was hovering around in the foyer when I arrived."

"Collinson has twisted his ankle." Lady Penridding sounded concerned and aggrieved at the same time. "Couldn't have happened at a worse time. Of course, he really isn't up to the job any longer, but I haven't the heart to turn him off. The man you saw is a temporary replacement, but he won't do."

"Is my wife here?" Theo cut in as though he could put off the question no longer.

"No. She is not. We did not, after all, expect you."

He felt his anger rising. "I trust she is in good hands. It seems to me, ma'am, that you have been permitting Pilar altogether too much license recently!"

"Hold your tongue, Theo! You are in no position, let me remind you, to cast stones! Had you behaved as you should toward Pilar, her well-being would not have become my concern!"

"That is all very fine, but . . ."

"But nothing!" snapped the old lady. "I'll not suffer your criticism. As it happens, Pilar is at present out shopping with my good friend Mrs. Beaumont, whose daughter Mary is much Pilar's age. Do you suppose I would permit the least hint of indiscretion to attach to the child while she is in my charge?"

Theo tossed off his drink and poured another. "No, but when I hear my wife's name bandied about in company, I may perhaps be forgiven for wondering!"

"Bandied about?" Lady Penridding raised a quizzing glass in one clawed hand to peer at him. "In what connection?" she demanded.

"For one thing, it appears she did not lack for escorts in Paris?"

"Are you referring to young Hammell?"

"And Staveley—so I heard."

She gave a sharp crack of laughter. "Someone has been busy! My dear boy, we didn't see Francis Staveley above twice. I believe he accompanied us to the theater. As for Roger, you should be grateful to him—his presence in Paris was invaluable—relieved me of much responsibility. And he proved a good friend to Pilar when her confidence needed to be restored."

She peered at him again and added with surprising mildness, "I must say, for someone who professes he don't give a jot, you're behaving irrationally. A little gratitude might not come amiss. I think you should be pleased with Pilar—she has come on a lot—blossomed. I have grown very fond of her."

Theo looked uncomfortable. "You have been very good, Grandmamma," he said stiffly. "And I'm sure you meant it all for the best. . . ."

"Don't be patronizing, m'boy—it don't become you! I don't know what plans you had made, but I will not tell you what you are going to do. You are going to close up Arlington Street and move in here. No!" She jangled an imperative hand. "Don't interrupt! Letty is to have her come-out this Season, I don't care for the child—never have—but I am not one to shirk my duty, and I can do no less for Letty than I did for her sister!"

"Forgive me, ma'am, but you have lost me!" Theo said irritably. "How will my removing here help you to do your duty by Letty, for I tell you plainly, I'll not lift one finger on Letty's behalf."

"That is for your own conscience to determine. However, you will take your place here as Pilar's husband—a role which has concerned you little until now!" He looked up angrily. "I will engage to present Pilar when I present Letty—but if we are to avoid unpleasant gossip, the family must show a united front to the world."

Theo strode across to the table and poured another glass of Madeira. She watched him, her glance softening. How he had always hated to be coerced! And how she loved him—willful, arrogant, infuriatingly stubborn boy! All her own worst faults, as she knew only too well! Just as she knew that if he loved, it would be in the same headlong fashion. If only he would love Pilar!

Nothing showed in her face, however, as he turned hard eyes to her. "And if I decline? And take Pilar away?"

"I hope you will not be so foolhardy! I have no wish to trouble your grandfather with matters which would distress him. Gout makes his temper very uncertain these days . . . he might take it into his head to withdraw the generous allowance which supplements your income—and, no doubt, pays for many of your pleasures."

They regarded one another with equal resolution until finally a gleam of respect came into Theo's eyes.

"Blackmail, ma'am?" he suggested sarcastically.

"If that is how you choose to call it," she returned with equanimity. "I prefer to term it 'gentle inducement.' "

He laughed abruptly, made her an exaggerated leg, and swung around to stare out of the window, struggling to come to terms with a good grace with the unpleasant sensation of having been routed.

Behind him, the door flew open to admit a slim whirlwind!

"Oh Lady Pen. You *are* here! What do you think! We have met the Duchess of Devonshire. She was most kind, and has invited me to go with her to Chiswick for the coming weekend! Do you suppose. . . ?"

The words trailed away on a gasp as the figure by the window turned.

"Georgy Devonshire!" drawled Theo. "You *are* flying high!"

Pilar's eyes, grown suddenly blank, sought Lady Penridding, who saw in that instant the whole of the girl's feelings laid bare. Mercy on us! It was worse than she had supposed! She nodded encouragement and, as though it were some kind of signal, Pilar seemed to gather herself. She extended a limp hand and sank into a curtsy.

"La, Theo! Is it really you?" she said with considerable composure. "We had quite given you up."

Theo put up his glass to survey his wife, and found the blood beating in his veins. His memory still carried a picture of Pilar as he had left her—dispirited, defeated.

Nothing could be further from his imaginings than this modish creature in a parma violet redingote of rustling taffeta—the wide Vandyke collar spilling over in soft falls of lace—her face a little pale beneath the outrageously stylish *chapeau à calotte* of puffed white gauze interlaced with violet ribbon.

He raised her up, retaining his hold on her. "I came in search of an errant wife," he said softly.

"Indeed, senor?" Her composure cracked a little. She tried to remove her hand, a spot of color high on each cheek. "A pity! An' you had valued her more highly, she might never have fled!"

His eyes glinted appreciatively. "You've not lost your sharp tongue, I see. Are you ready to return home?"

"Oh, but . . ." She stopped, made a determined effort to release her hand, and stepped away from him. "You may do as you please," she said loftily. "I am content where I am. We have a ball planned and many other things, Lady Pen and I. She will be very pleased for me to stay, I think."

She whisked across the room to perch on the arm of Lady Penridding's chair. The old lady noted the obstinate set of the full red mouth—and made her voice deliberately stern.

"Of course, it would grieve me greatly to lose you, Pilar, particularly now with the deplorable

Gertrude and her offspring about to descend upon me, but nonetheless you will obey your husband."

"Even if he is unreasonable?"

"My love—husbands are frequently unreasonable. It is one of the crosses a wife must bear. Equally, they may sometimes be disposed to be generous." Lady Penridding reached up to tweak the stubborn chin and looked steadily at her grandson.

He read the message and bowed sardonically. "So be it, Gran. I'll play your little game, but don't complain if I come to blows with Gertrude! Oh, and if you mean to entertain in prime style, you had best have Meecham in place of Collinson."

The door opened to admit Sir Roger Hammell. He saw Theo and halted on the threshold in almost comical confusion. "Oh lor!" he muttered.

There was an awkward silence. Pilar looked from one to the other—and half-rose.

"Oh, please . . ." she began anxiously.

"Well? Are you going to stand there forever like a couple of game cocks sizing one another up!" demanded Lady Penridding.

Theo grinned suddenly and held out a hand. "A truce, Ham? No pistols at dawn, I entreat you! It would grieve me greatly to put a bullet in you."

Sir Roger beamed and seized the proferred hand, pumping it up and down with obvious relief.

"*Muy bien!*" said Pilar, satisfied.

12

Theo moved into Berkeley Square and found his new Pilar a tantalizing creature, mercurial, out-going, surprisingly confident, and already much in demand.

He was at first amused and then piqued that she seemed to have so little need of him. It was a new experience for Theo—and one that he found exasperating. Pilar was not distant—in fact she took a delight in teasing him—but they were seldom alone, and when they were, she would not be serious.

No doubt it was a situation he could have remedied with a little forceful persuasion, but pride stood in his way—for the first time in his life he feared rejection. And so, although he played the dutiful husband when his grandmother required it of him, he still went very much his own way.

The advent of the Dowager Lady Gilmore and Letty did little to ease matters. Gertrude very quickly made her presence felt. Finding Pilar so popular, she lost no time in voicing her opinions to Lady Penridding.

"It seems quite extraordinary to me, the way Pilar has insinuated herself into the Devonshire House set. I am surprised that you condone such a connection. The Duchess is incorrigibly fast, and who are her friends, pray? Fox, who as everyone knows is up to his ears in debt—and a tame Irish playwriter and his singing wife . . . fine company, indeed!"

"And Lady Melbourne—and the Prince of Wales! Don't forget him," said the old lady spitefully. "Such a charming young man. . . ."

"It will turn Pilar's head!" But already Gertrude's manner was less forceful as the implications of the situation began to present themselves.

"Pilar is a married woman," said her ladyship flatly. "It is not for me to choose her friends. The Duchess has been very kind—and the Prince has shown a decided liking for Pilar."

"Of course, your Whig sympathies are well known," said Gertrude with a contemptible lack of subtlety, "and while I cannot share them, I should not object if Letty should sometimes be invited to accompany her sister-in-law."

With something suspiciously like a snort, Lady Penridding said dryly, "I thought you couldn't stomach Pilar at any price?"

"I make no secret of my dislike—and disapproval. In my opinion, Theo was mad not to have Arren's girl. Poor child, she took his rejection very hard. Her mother finally had to carry her home to Cornwall." Gertrude was stiff with outrage. "I shall be a long time forgiving Theo for the invidious position in which I was placed. However, his marriage is a fact, and since you have seen fit to take Pilar up, my opinion obviously counts for very little. I can only trust you may never have cause to regret the time and trouble you have lavished upon her!"

Lady Penridding rose from her chair with a discordant jangle of bracelets. "You, of all people, Gertrude, should know that I never waste time in repining!"

Gertrude's lips thinned to a sharp line, but she said no more.

It began as a scurrilous morsel of gossip confided across coffeehouse tables; from there it spread to the gaming houses and was soon being hinted at behind fans in plump-cushioned drawing rooms. Inevitably word reached the ear of Georgiana, Duchess of Devonshire, who lost no time in passing it on to the person most concerned.

"I am sorry," said Pilar. "I can quite see that such scandals must not be permitted to attach to your home and friends. I will not come again."

Georgiana burst out laughing. "My dear—I don't give a fig for scandal! I have always known about the little episode at Rackam's. Charles told me—and I found it excessively diverting. But this!" her dark blue eyes were alight with the joy of conspiracy. "Is it true? You really are a gypsy?"

Pilar nodded, mutely.

"But how romantic! And you truly don't know your father's identity? Oh, heavens, I declare, I haven't been so entertained for years." She saw Pilar's misery and her voice softened. "Listen, my dear. I will tell you about gossip. You can deny it at great length and everyone will at once know it to be the truth. Or you can hide yourself away, as I think perhaps you intend—and the result will be much the same, except that the world will despise you even more!"

Pilar's head came up angrily.

"Or, you can admit to the whole story—embellish it if you've a mind—laugh into their silly, shocked faces, and soon they will begin to wonder if perhaps it is not just a huge practical joke! And lest they are made to look foolish, most will drop the whole subject!"

"You really think this?" Pilar looked unconvinced.

Georgiana's laughter was brittle. "I know it. Has the news reached Lady Penridding? No? Then tell her, ask her if I am not right. In fact," she sprang up from the sofa where they sat, chestnut curls bouncing, "I think we should go even further." The blue eyes were burning now with mischief. "I shall arrange a masked ball at Chiswick next month, and you shall come as a gypsy!"

It wasn't long before the rumors reached Theo. He was furious and immediately settled blame where he was convinced it belonged.

"Don't be a ninnyhammer!" scoffed Sir Roger. "Letty ain't got the brains to lay such an insidious trail of venom. You'll need to look in quite another direction."

"Such as?"

Sir Roger looked as though he was already regretting his impetuous outburst, but Theo pressed him.

"Come on, Ham. You had much better tell me."

"You won't like it," Sir Roger said bluntly.

"Who, Ham?" Theo's voice was grim.

"*Cherchez la femme*, dear boy!" Ham mumbled miserably. "A jealous female can be the very devil!"

"You mean . . . ? Oh, good God—not Suzanne?" Theo looked stunned. "No! You must be mistaken!"

"Wish I was, dear boy. Hadn't meant to blab, but there is every reason to suppose that she was behind that disastrous episode at Rackam's. Sheridan swore he'd seen her setting the whole thing up—didn't realize the significance until later."

"But—how would Suzanne know the rest? No one knew outside our own immediate household— and I would vouch for them, every one."

Sir Roger shrugged. "A trip to Yorkshire . . . a few pertinent questions ventured here and there. Easiest thing in the world to accomplish if you've a mind!"

Theo's interview with Mrs. Verney was painfully brief. He pushed past the servant who would have him announced and surprised her in her shell-pink boudoir, still *en déshabille*, with her red hair rippling loose over a silk négligé. He cut short her pleasure on seeing him.

She denied all knowledge of the scandal, but not for long against his damning evidence to the contrary. She pleaded, cajoled, and finding him implacable, was reduced at last to tears and finally to abuse.

He heard her out in stony silence, sickened and appalled.

"I advise you to repair at once to your 'relation' in Paris," he said when she paused for breath. "For an indefinite stay."

Suzanne's bosom heaved angrily. "You have no right. . . ."

"If you stay here," he continued silkily, "I shall make it my business to have every door of any significance closed to you. Oh yes, I can do it—if you doubt my ability, stay and you will see!"

"You are a devil!" she cried and then, frightened by his expression, "I cannot afford to live abroad!"

He tossed a bag of guineas on the bed contemptuously. "That should start you off. I'm sure you'll soon find consolation!"

He had no way of knowing whether Pilar had heard the rumors—and since Penridding House was in a state of upheaval in preparation for the ball and tempers were balanced on a hairline, it hardly seemed the time to broach the matter.

To Pilar's delight, Adam came to Town and confessed himself enchanted with her and pleased by her success.

Her gown for the ball, of champagne figured silk over pale gauze petticoats, turned her skin to gold and her hair, dressed by Lady Penridding's own coiffeur, was powdered for the first time since her return from Paris; the effect was quite lovely, making her eyes sparkle like black jewels. Theo found his eyes returning to her time and again at dinner and later during the reception.

Leading her out for the opening dance, he murmured under cover of the music, "Well-madam wife?"

"Well, husband?"

"Are you content to be the most captivating woman in the room?"

Her heart leaped, but she only touched his ruby coat. "*Gracias*. You are very fine also, I think."

"I have seen you very little of late," he said abruptly.

"Oh, I am having a splendid time! And it is quite the thing for husbands and wives to lead separate lives, you know. Georgiana hardly ever sees the Duke!"

His step and bow were mockingly exaggerated. Their fingers touched again. "Thank you, *querida*, for explaining the niceties of our society life!"

Pilar flushed and tossed her head. "I forget how well versed you are! But the rules are sometimes silly. It is a pity that your Suzanne was not invited for this evening. I should not have minded in the least, you understand, but Grandmother was shocked!"

"I bet she was!" he laughed angrily. "Anyway, Mrs. Verney would not have come. She has gone abroad—for her health!"

Adam, sitting with Lady Penridding, watched their graceful progress down the room.

"They make a handsome pair."

"Humph! Handsome is as handsome does!" her ladyship sniffed. "Still, I'll allow they look well enough—even in a gathering as impressive as this."

"It is impressive, isn't it? Even Aunt Gertrude must be gratified. I see Letty has Forton for a partner."

"Oh, Gertrude will find something to complain of. Unfortunately Letty is taken with young Gervaise Beaumont and that won't suit! He'll be well enough breeched in due course, but nothing less than an Earldom will do for Gertrude."

She observed a slim elderly man in lavender silk approaching. "Oh drat! Here is Horry Walpole come to quizz me about Pilar. He's like a dog with a bone when he senses a mystery! There are times when it becomes very tiresome knowing so little of the child's parentage. It is so much easier to lie convincingly if one knows exactly what it is one wishes to conceal."

Adam laughed and moved away, after greeting Mr. Walpole and inquiring after his health.

Pilar was leaving the floor with Theo, who at once relinquished her and sauntered away. Adam could hardly fail to observe the wistful glance that followed him.

"Well, my dear? Are you enjoying your evening?"

"Oh, yes. It is all very nice."

"You don't sound exactly overjoyed."

Pilar gave herself a little shake. "That is because I am being stupid, for it is stupid to not be content with all this."

"Theo?" he asked gently.

"Oh, we are very civilized when we are together. But that is not often, unless Lady Penridding insists that he accompany us to the theater or a party. . . ." Her voice said it all.

Adam wondered if it were wise to offer hope. "Perhaps that is at the root of it," he ventured. "Theo always did hate being compelled to do anything."

"Do you really think it?" Her eagerness made Adam furious with Theo, but before he could say more she was running on: "Letty looks well, don't you think? White becomes her fairness and she is not so bad as her mother. And I must tell you that Ham is falling in love with Mary Beaumont! I teased him about it yesterday and he blushed. And tonight he has hardly taken his eyes from her."

"Mary Beaumont!" Adam was diverted. "After all his amours? Why, she is quite a plain little thing!"

"Oh, but she is nice! I do not care for my sex much, but I like Mary. And she will be very good for Ham, I think."

It was well into the evening when Mr. Fox approached Lady Penridding and bent over her hand. At his shoulder was a gentleman she recognized as Mr. Staveley's brother.

"Forgive my lateness, dear lady. I was detained on important business. You know Lord Ardwicke? He has just returned from America and as I am impatient to hear all his news, I ventured to bring him along."

Lady Penridding made his lordship welcome, eyeing him with some curiosity. He had aged little since they had last met; he must be about forty now, she supposed—a handsome, pleasant man of average height, a bit of a dandy in his dress but without the excesses of his more flamboyant friend. There were tired lines about his eyes, but with the grace of the true diplomat he made her feel that his only wish in life was to please her.

"And how are things in America, Lord Ard-wicke?" She signed him to the chair at her side.

Lord Ardwicke crossed one leg over the other. "When I left, Clinton had Charlestown under seige—and was endeavoring to cut communications with the North. If he succeeds, Charlestown will be ours by now." He saw Fox's face. "My dear Charles, we are at war and must fight!"

"We could sue for peace!"

Lord Ardwicke glanced significantly at his hostess. "Ma'am, your pardon. We grow too serious for the occasion. Your grandson is married, Charles tells me."

Pilar was dancing with Mr. Staveley when the natural rhythm of his step faltered and he drew in a sharp breath.

Pilar looked up at him. "Why, senor? Is something amiss?"

"Forgive me," he said slowly. "I was taken aback." He glanced down at her, his manner a trifle abstracted. "I was not aware that my brother was invited for this evening. I had not even supposed him to be in the country."

Her brow puckered. "You have a brother?"

"Indeed I have. He is at this moment engaging Lady Penridding in conversation."

Pilar cast a discreet glance in their direction. "How is it that I have not known?"

"He is some years my senior—and far more . . . worthy!" Francis Staveley's lip curled in self-mocking. "A diplomat and a champion of lost causes!"

"You do not like him, I think?"

"We are not . . . intimate!" he said softly.

The music ended. As they quit the floor, Lady Penridding beckoned.

"Lord Ardwicke, may I present my grandson's wife."

Pilar spread her skirts and gave him her hand. He saluted her with grave courtesy and looked up into Mr. Staveley's mocking eyes.

"Your servant, brother Harry."

"Francis." The Earl's voice was still pleasant, but cooler. "I hope I find you well?"

"Tolerable, brother. And you?"

"Thank you, yes. A little tired." he turned back to Pilar, who was wondering if she was alone in feeling the tension beneath the pleasantries. Quite unbidden, old Ursula's words came back to her. "You will set brother against brother. . . ." No, that was too silly!

"Lady Gilmore? May I hope for the pleasure of a dance?" Lord Ardwicke was speaking and she shook off the shadows from the past.

"If you would like it, senor," she said shyly, and saw Mr. Staveley's lips tighten.

"Have you been long in England, Lady Gilmore?" the Earl asked when they were presently going down the dance.

Pilar had told the small lie so often that it came

almost without thought, yet suddenly she found herself faltering over the words. His manner, however, was kindly, as though he found her hesitation perfectly natural in the circumstances, which only confused her the more.

The dance parted them and when they came together again, he directed the conversation to an account of his travels, relating only the lighter moments for her amusement, and they parted on a most agreeable note, with Pilar wondering how Mr. Staveley could so dislike his brother.

It was past three o'clock in the morning before the last carriage rattled away from Penridding House, leaving behind a strong feeling of anticlimax—the empty rooms still ringing to the echoes of ghostly laughter and gaiety.

Lady Penridding declared herself well satisfied, but seemed abstracted as she mounted the stairs with weary tread. Gertrude, by contrast, was positively glowing with satisfaction. Lord Montague had stood up twice with Letty and had been heard to express his intention of calling on the following day. Since the size of his lordship's fortune was in keeping with his girth, Gertrude's mind was already dwelling on bridals!

Pilar, noting Letty's air of preoccupation during her mother's peroration, guessed that her thoughts were centered on Gervaise Beaumont. For the first time she felt a measure of sympathy for her spoilt, pretty sister-in-law.

For herself, the evening had been one of almost unqualified triumph, marred only by Theo's disappearance into the card room soon after supper. He had stayed only long enough to hear the lovely voice of Elizabeth Sheridan, who had once been Elizabeth Linley and a famous singer, and whose marriage to her beloved "*cheri*" had been even more romantic and extraordinary than hers to Theo. But Elizabeth Sheridan was cherished and loved!

The thought unsettled Pilar, left her restless and cross. As Amy undressed her and set about the tedious task of brushing her hair free of powder, she pushed the hairbrush aside and sprang to her feet.

While Amy hovered in consternation, she dragged a riding habit from the closet.

"Oh, milady! You're never going to . . . not in the middle of the night!"

"On the contrary, it is almost morning and I shall never sleep! It is already much too hot, and this room suffocates me! Besides, I have ridden out more than once while you slept!"

"Oh, ma'am! You didn't ought! Really you didn't!"

"My good Amy! Fasten me up and then go to bed and do not be so foolish! There is never anyone to see me. I am quite safe."

There was a faint lightening in the sky when she slid from Mayfly's back at last in the warm, shuffling darkness of the mews stable where a solitary lamp glowed dimly.

"Dickon," she called softly, "I am returned."

"If Dickon is your tame stable lad," said Theo, stepping out of the blackness beyond the light, "I have sent him back to his bed."

"You!" Pilar had never seen him so casually dressed, with coat and vest discarded and his shirt opened carelessly to the waist. Her heart began to race. "Why are you here?"

"I'm waiting for you, my dear. I came to your room, but found my bird had flown." He took Mayfly's rein from her unresisting fingers and led the little mare into her stall, threw a blanket over her, and came out, latching the door.

Pilar stood, uncertain whether to go or stay, but even as she battled with her wildly conflicting emotions, the decision was out of her hands. She was drawn inexorably into the pool of light.

"Your popularity tonight has been quite prodigious. You find me suffering the pangs of neglect."

"That is not true!" she protested. "You were nowhere to be seen!"

Theo smiled, but there was a hardness in his eyes. "Nevertheless, I am entitled to some measure of your time . . . and when better to claim it than now? Did you enjoy your ride?"

"Very much!" she said defiantly.

"I see! And do you often cavort about the streets in the middle of the night?"

"Not often."

"But when you have cause?" His grip tightened. "A secret assignation, perhaps?"

"No! You know I would not!" Pilar struggled to free herself. "It is only that sometimes, even now, I get this feeling inside me—and I must answer it!"

The intensity in her voice made him look closer, his own pulses quickening. "Why, what is this?" He cupped her face in his hands, turning it up to the light. "So, my little gypsy is not quite lost to me, after all!"

His kiss was everything she had longed for, and for a long, treacherous moment she succumbed.

"Ah, how I have missed you!" he murmured against her mouth, and tasted the salt of her tears. He thrust her away, his eyes raking her. "You are crying!"

"I am *estúpida*! But if you break my heart again,

I think I shall not bear it! Suzanne . . ." her voice broke on the hated name.

"Forget Suzanne!" he said abruptly and then, seeing her flinch, he drew her forward into his arms, but gently, and held her, his cheek against her hair. "Suzanne no longer holds any part of me, *querida*. God knows, I have been the stupid one! I can only regret that it took me so long to realize it!"

Pilar was having difficulty with her breathing. "Are you saying that you love me?"

"*Con toda mi alma!*" he said in a shaking voice. "Will you give me the chance to prove it to you?" He kissed her again with lingering gentleness. "We don't have to go back to the house." Theo seized her hand and led her to a far stall filled with fresh, sweet hay. "What do you say to that for a bed? Or are you now grown too nice in your notions?"

"No!" she protested, half-laughing. "But—oh, *mi esposo*, you are quite mad! We will be discovered!"

"What of it! It will give them something to scandalize over below stairs . . . confirm to them what they have always known—that we are all mad! I am willing to chance it if you are. Besides," he murmured persuasively, "I have never tumbled a girl in the hay! You would be filling a sad gap in my education and give me something to boast of to my grandsons in my dotage!"

Pilar, suddenly all gypsy, said boldly, "It is a confident man, lord, who speaks of grandsons when he has not yet fathered his first born!"

"An' you are willing, my wife," he answered in like vein, "that is an omission I mean to rectify with all speed!"

She gurgled with laughter, which stilled as

suddenly as it began. Her eyes were very black in the lamplight. "You are sure, *amigo*?"

For an answer he seized her in a crushing embrace and, as her body yielded deliciously and her arms came up around his neck to hold him closer, he lifted her and strode forward, putting out a hand to the lamp as he passed. The flame flickered once and went out.

13

Pilar was happier than she had ever thought possible—so happy that she was almost afraid, and stored each moment against the future.

The changed situation was spectacularly obvious to Lady Penridding when she summoned them both to her room on the morning following the ball. She was still abed, though her face was painted and every hair of her wig in place. She sat upright in the huge bed amid a pile of lace pillows, tired but indomitable.

"You are looking remarkably smug this morning, Theo," she observed.

"He has discovered that he loves me," Pilar explained dreamily.

"Has he?" Her laugh cracked. "Well, I never thought him a slow top, but in this instance I almost despaired of him!" She gave them both a searching glance. "I'm loath to bring you down from that peak of ecstasy, but Mr. Walpole told me last evening of some rather disquieting rumors which are circulating."

"Trust Horry Walpole to be first with the news. I had hoped to keep it from you. Yes, Gran," Theo said dryly, "the story is going around that I was tricked into marriage with a gypsy!"

She looked sharply at Pilar, but the child seemed

undismayed. "But how? Was it Gertrude . . . or Letty?"

"Neither, Gran. I regret it was Mrs. Verney." Theo had the grace to look uncomfortable as he related what had passed.

Again Lady Penridding's eyes went to Pilar, but she only grinned. "Last week I would have killed her with my own hands! Now, I do not care. She has lost Theo. That is punishment enough, I think!"

Theo said, "I don't know how Suzanne found out so much, Gran!"

"That hardly matters now, my boy," she said severely. "You will have to accustom yourselves to a degree of notoriety."

"The Duchess says we should tell everyone it is true," said Pilar. "Except that I did not trick Theo, of course . . . and that we should laugh when they are scandalized. She said you would agree with her."

"Did she, indeed!" The old lady's finely plucked brows disappeared into her hair. "Huh! I always have thought Georgiana a flighty, impetuous creature—forever rushing into causes! I suppose this is all of a piece with the rest! But I'll thank her not to make me a party to her crack-brained notions!"

"Well, I think she's right, Gran," said Theo, sprawling in a chair with what she considered to be a shocking lack of concern. "After all, there's little sport to be had from baiting a willing victim."

"Oh. You'll do as you please, I've no doubt!" Lady Penridding sniffed and hunched into her pillows, disapproving of their laxity, and therefore unwilling to extend any but the most grudging approval. "I'm too old for all these complicated stratagems. I just hope you know what you're doing!"

"It will be all right," Pilar consoled her. "You will see."

This buoyant mood continued over the days that followed. It soon became apparent to all that the Gilmores, whatever had been assumed to the contrary, were very much in love and highly entertained by the notion that Theo had in any way been coerced into marriage; his lordship's amused acceptance of his wife's gypsy origins confused the issue further, so that in a very short space of time, as predicted, the tongues ceased to wag so freely, and with the exception of a few coldly turned shoulders the affair was all but forgotten and a new topic emerged to enslave the gossip mongers.

Parliament was preparing to debate an Act rescinding some of the old Penal laws against Roman Catholics. It was a Bill very close to Charles Fox's heart, and the Duchess of Devonshire and all her friends threw themselves wholeheartedly into canvassing for him—and deploring the antics of the fanatical Lord George Gordon, who opposed the Bill at every turn.

Tempers grew short as the June days grew longer and hotter. Pilar and Theo took to riding very early in the mornings when the streets were deserted except for an occasional tradesman or the tired, plodding chairmen carrying home some tardy reveler, and when the cool green parks were heavy with dew and empty of all but birdsong.

And on one of these rides, when Pilar had grown complacent in her love, a shot fired from one of Hyde Park's more secluded walks missed her by a hair's breadth and struck Theo in the upper arm.

"The devil!" he swore, clapping a hand over the

spreading stain on his sleeve. His keen eyes swept the park urgently for signs of movement. "Get out of here, *querida*! If they mean business, they'll try again! Go—quickly, now!"

The blood had drained from her face, but she was very calm as her eyes sought his. "Certainly not. Are you able to ride, *mi esposo*, if I lead you?"

"I'm all right, and you're wasting valuable time! Do as I ask, Pilar, for the love of God! You can send someone to me. Just go!"

"No. It will be much better if I do not leave you. We will go together." She brought the little mare in close and grasped his rein firmly.

There came the sound of galloping behind them. Pilar drew a swift breath and heard Theo's groan of angry frustration. Her breath came a little quicker, but she did not tell him of the knife comfortingly secured against her leg. If she must, she would use it—but if there should be more than one assailant. . . ?

"Lady Gilmore? My lord? Are you all right? I thought I heard a shot!"

Unbelievably, it was Mr. Staveley. He took in the situation at a glance and ranged himself without fuss on Theo's other side. Together the three made slow progress.

"Was it footpads?"

"We saw nothing," Pilar confessed, tremulous in her relief. "But one supposes your coming must have put them to flight."

"Then I am glad to have been of some small service."

Theo's face was by now ashen; he swayed drunkenly in the saddle.

"Forgive me, my lord, but should you not dismount and rest? It would take but a few minutes for me to ride on to Penridding House and bring back a carriage."

"Thank you, Staveley, but I'll do as I am."

"As you wish."

Pilar gave Theo a helpless look that deplored his stubbornness and turned impulsively to Mr. Staveley. "We are in your debt, senor. If you had not come when you did . . ." she could not bring herself to finish the sentence. "You do not usually ride so early, I think?"

"No. It was pure chance. Like yourselves, I imagine—foreseeing another hot day, I thought to take some air while it still retained a little freshness. And I thank God for't."

Back at Penridding House, Theo was got to bed in a surprisingly short space of time and the doctor sent for. Pilar was not impressed by the stout, pompous Dr. Morant, and resisted all attempts to wrest her from Theo's side. With Adam at her shoulder, she stood stiffly beside the bed with her hand crushed in Theo's good one. Her arrogant, impassive stare unnerved the doctor somewhat, but he removed the bullet competently enough and in spite of her protests, bled his patient, and left him weak and already drowsy with laudanum.

Later, when they were alone, she lifted frightened eyes to Fredericks, who was almost as pale as his master.

"He will not die?"

"Oh, no, my lady! I have every confidence that we shall pull him through."

"It will be no thanks to that *leech*!" she said pugnaciously. "He is like a great, overstuffed pudding!"

"Dr. Morant is very well thought of, my lady.

And sleep is a great healer." The valet looked at her keenly. "Perhaps, if you were to take a little rest yourself . . . and you have not eaten, I think? The laudanum will render his lordship insensible for some hours."

"Thank you, but I prefer to stay. I could not eat."

Later in the day, Lady Penridding came rustling into the room to say that Mr. Staveley was below.

"I think you should see him, child. He seemed most concerned—for you as well as for Theo—and we do owe him a great debt of gratitude. If he had not come along just when he did, things might have been so much worse!" She looked toward the bed where Theo lay restlessly dozing. The morning's events had shaken her badly. She still exuded her habitual air of positiveness, but beneath the rouge her face was gray and for the first time Pilar thought that her years betrayed her.

In Lady Penridding's drawing room, golden with sunlight streaming between half drawn curtains, Francis Staveley came forward and took Pilar's hand. "I will not keep you above a minute, but I could not rest until I had assured myself that Lord Gilmore was on the road to recovery?"

"Thank you. The bullet is out and everyone is confident that he will mend." Her words lacked conviction.

Mr. Staveley had brought roses—pink ones, masses of them—and Pilar buried her face in them to shut out the picture of Theo as she had left him, all his restless vitality dissipated into a frustrated raging against his confinement, which in turn left him weak.

For the rest of that day and all through the night

she stayed beside him while his wound grew angry and throbbed and his fever mounted. In one of his more lucid moments he peered at her and muttered fretfully, "It's dark, *hija* . . . you should be in your bed! All this nonsense. . . !"

"Not at all, *mi esposo*," Pilar returned calmly. "I am where I wish to be. And besides, I slept for a whole two hours earlier this evening when Adam sat with you; now Fredericks is taking his rest. That poor man's devotion to you is something to behold, so you must be good and get well!"

But Theo was no better when Fredericks touched her shoulder to wake her from a light doze as dawn came slanting through the shades. And when Adam came in and observed the unnatural brilliance of his eyes, he said curtly that the doctor must be summoned at once.

"No!" Pilar cried, and filled with a sudden cold terror, she rushed from the room.

Fredericks said quietly, "Her ladyship is taking it hard."

Adam frowned and hurried after her, but she was nowhere to be found.

It was more than an hour later, when the doctor's chaise was at the door, that she came flying up the stairs past an astonished Meecham, dignity abandoned, hair streaming out, and skirts lifted, in disarray, and flung open the door of Theo's bedchamber. Four heads turned in varying degrees of surprise and annoyance.

Dr. Morant was already bending over his patient with Fredericks at his side, bowl at the ready. Adam, too, was there. And Theo's grandmother, roused by all the commotion. She hovered anxiously near the bed, tinier than ever in a voluminous wrap and looking curiously foreshortened without her wig, the sharp-featured face, unpainted and grown wizened with worry, wrapped around by a lacy bedbonnet.

Pilar advanced determinedly upon the doctor. "You!" she accused. "You will not lay one more finger on my husband!"

"Pilar!" cried Lady Penridding.

The doctor looked vaguely apoplectic, but struggled to make allowances for a wife's natural anguish. "Ma'am . . . this is most distressing for you! Might I suggest . . ."

"No, you might not," she said flatly. "I would like you to leave now and not to come back!"

"My dear Pilar, you are being unreasonable," said Adam quietly. "You must allow the doctor to know what he is about."

"Precisely!" The doctor's tone was unctuous, patronizing. "You see, dear lady, his lordship has a high fever. He must be bled."

Pilar darted forward, black eyes flashing, and seized his knife, waving it threateningly under his nose. "If you do not leave this instant, I will bleed *you*!"

From then on, the situation rapidly deteriorated into chaos, with Adam clinging desperately to reason, Lady Penridding arguing furiously, and the doctor, under the threat of intimidation from that unwavering blade and assailed by a stream of Spanish invective, hastily packing his bag.

"She's unhinged!" he spluttered to Lady Penridding. "Never have I been so treated! I feel obliged to say that if Lord Gilmore's condition worsens, as it must . . ."

"My husband will not die!" Pilar stated haughtily, "Because I do not let him die! From now—I, his wife, look after him!"

"Oh, good God!" The roused passions had penetrated Theo's fevered brain; the voice from the bed, though weak, was lucid and held the ghost of a laugh. "So you have me a helpless victim, at last, little savage . . . I believe you will greatly enjoy practicing your damned Romany arts on me!"

Pilar thrust the knife back into the doctor's hand, looking contemptuous as he flinched involuntarily. And then she forgot him as she rushed across to kneel beside Theo, taking his hand and covering it with fierce kisses. "Do not listen to them! I will make you well, *mi esposo . . . mi queridisimo amigo*! Already Cook is preparing a draught which will bring down your fever. It is not easy in London to find the plants that I need, but I searched and I found them, so you may be easy!"

Theo choked on a feeble laugh and closed his eyes in mock resignation. At once she looked anxious. "You trust me?"

"With my life," he sighed, opening his eyes again. They were bright with pain as they lifted to the much abused Morant, who had been staring in disbelief at what he heard. "You have offended the good doctor, little *malvada*! You must forgive my wife, Morant . . . she is something out of the common, as you will have noted! But she has a talent . . . and I believe I must indulge her. . . ." He was already finding concentration difficult.

"As you will, my lord!" The plump little man was rigid with disapproval. He glared at Pilar, who glared back. "I shall not remain one moment longer where I am plainly not wanted." He turned to Lady Penridding and added significantly, "Should you further require the services of a physician, ma'am," his tone indicated that she most certainly would, "may I suggest that you seek them elsewhere."

"Well!" declared Lady Penridding when Adam had ushered Dr. Morant from the room. "I hope we may not have cause to rue this day's work! It's my belief that you have both taken leave of your senses!"

On the third day, Lady Penridding emerged into the room and stared at the foot of that bed. Theo seemed worse in her.

"Go on, Gertrude," ... Pilar, quick, ... and watched, Pilar ... to a vague ease when ... He put out his good arm to draw Pilar close and ... ... rested her head against his shoulder, in an ... anxious gesture of ... Her hair was ... ... against his ... nipped and his other outstretched.

14

As the time for the Duchess of Devonshire's masquerade ball drew nearer, Theo was already well on the road to recovery, and Pilar was once more restored to his grandmother's good graces.

There had been a coolness on Lady Penridding's part ever since that disastrous scene in Theo's room—a coolness which Gertrude was quick to note and happy to endorse. But her snubs went unheeded, for Pilar, totally absorbed in the task of restoring her husband to health, would scarcely have noticed, or cared, if the whole world had turned against her.

The vile herbal potions, the leaves of coltsfoot so assiduously gathered, first by herself and then by the ever-faithful Amy, made into an ointment and applied to Theo's arm in place of the well-tried poultices, were viewed by all with unconcealed dismay; even Fredericks, at times, found his loyalty stretched to the limit.

Only Theo, cursing her remedies with an admirable fluency in lucidity and delirium alike, reposed in her his entire confidence; and in a remarkably short space of time that confidence was rewarded; his fever diminished steadily and the festering wound began to heal.

On the third day, Lady Penridding stomped into the room and stood at the foot of the bed. Theo grinned weakly at her.

"You see, Gran—a regular Devil's child! Saved for eventual perdition by my own personal witch!"

He put out his good arm to draw Pilar close and she rested her head against his shoulder in an unconscious gesture of weariness. Her hair was simply tied back, and against its severity the bones of her face, finely sculpted and bloodless, stood out with a stark beauty; a strong, timeless face, the eyes darkly smudged.

Lady Penridding was overcome with guilt; she had thought she knew Pilar, but there were depths in the child she had not imagined until now; to her shame, she had made little attempt to understand those strange passions that drove her to do what must be done without counting the cost.

Theo kissed his wife and pushed her from him. "Take her away, Gran—and make her rest. I shall do very well, now."

"Yes," she said abruptly. "I can see that you will."

The old lady, unused to apologizing, tried to make her peace with Pilar when she had seen her safely tucked up in her bed, but Pilar, already hazy with sleep, only sounded bewildered.

"Why should you be sorry?" she murmured. "You did not understand that for me, it was very simple, for if Theo dies, then I die also." She was asleep even as she uttered the words, and Lady Penridding, gazing down on her through an uncharacteristic blur of tears, felt the old affection swell and grow into something deeper and more profound.

Theo's return to health was not achieved without

setbacks. As his condition improved, his temper worsened, and the constant stream of visitors and well-wishers, while keeping him occupied, left him more often than not, tired and irritable. Gertrude, with her appalling lack of sensitivity, exacerbated his condition on the only occasion she was permitted to visit him by lecturing him on the folly of associating with political agitators such as Fox and his ilk, folly to which she unswervingly ascribed his present misfortune. His retaliatory blast could be heard all over the house and set his recovery back by days!

It was a trying time for all, but especially for Pilar, who bore it well but grew noticeably taut. And when Adam, who had been a rock, was obliged to go into the country on a matter of some urgency, he urged her before leaving not to jeopardize her own health.

"I know Lady Penridding worries about you. You are looking tired—and over pale."

Pilar did not tell him of her sickness the last few mornings; she knew the signs well enough, and was pleased. But now was not the time to talk of babies.

"You must get out more," Adam was urging. "Theo won't have a relapse now. He has little patience, I know, but he must learn to do without you sometimes. It wouldn't do Letty any harm to sit with him occasionally."

He said much the same to Theo, but in rather stronger terms. His cousin acquiesced, grudgingly, but balked at the prospect of being ministered to by his sister.

However, Letty—removed from her mother's overbearing influence and softened by her growing attachment to Gervaise Beaumont—was a surprising success in the sickroom. Once they had overcome an initial reluctance—a suspicion of one another—brother and sister gradually established a kind of rapport. She refused to pander to his whims, and he found her pertness and naive chatter curiously refreshing. Soon she was confiding her fears about Lord Montague.

"I'll just die if Mamma forces me to marry him!" she wailed. "He is so *fat*—and he talks of nothing but his stomach and his wretched horses! Besides, he is all of thirty-five!"

Theo's lips twitched. "Whereas Gervaise Beaumont is a mere stripling of twenty-two!"

Letty blushed scarlet.

"So that's the way of it! Are you in love with Beaumont?"

"Really, Theo! I . . . we . . . that is . . ."

"Never mind," said Theo laconically. "I infer he is likewise smitten."

"He does quite like me, I believe," she stammered. "Oh, but he has behaved most properly! And anyway . . ." her voice quivered tragically, "Mamma would never permit it."

"No. She wouldn't, would she?" said Theo with a slow grin.

When Sir Roger next came to see him, he made him privy to his plans. Theo sat in a chair by the open window; Sir Roger perched on the sill.

"It shouldn't be too difficult, Ham. There's you and Beaumont's sister a regular pair of lovebirds, so I'm told . . . easy enough for you to make up a four."

"I haven't . . . Mary Beaumont is a very dear girl, but . . ." Ham was plainly embarrassed.

"Oh, good God, man, don't be coy! It's as plain as your nose you're head over ears in love! It must be a disease—we're all at it! Anyway, you are elected to help. I would dearly love to spike my stepmother's guns!"

He plucked at the blanket covering his knees with sudden irritability. "Deuce take it! I'm sick of stewing in this damned chair . . . time I was taking some exercise. Come on, Ham—help me up!"

"Whoa! Steady on the bit, old fellow! Wait a minute, now—do! Pilar said nothing about . . ."

"Pilar ain't here," Theo said abruptly. "If you're not disposed to help, I'll go it alone!"

"Lord, you're a stubborn man . . ." Sir Roger leaped forward as Theo came to his feet, and got a shoulder under him. In this fashion they staggered drunkenly around the room, with Theo panting and sweating profusely, and were caught like guilty children when Pilar arrived back unexpectedly early.

They were castigated unmercifully and Theo bundled back to his chair. She stood, hands on hips, surveying them both in a smoldering rage.

"Looks magnificent when she's angry, don't she, Ham?" gasped Theo, more exhausted than he was willing to admit.

"Don't you woo me with sweet words, *estúpido*!" she flashed back. "Look at you! No breath—and the sweat still pouring off you!"

"It is a very hot day, *hija*," Sir Roger pleaded unhappily.

"And don't you speak to me, either . . . traitor . . . conspirator. . . !"

"Enough, Pilar! Have done, for pity's sake!" Theo snapped. "I'm weak, that's all. You'd be weak, stuck in this accursed chair! I have to make a start sometime!"

Her eyes spat fire. "But when I, your wife, say so—and not before!"

There was a constraint between them for the rest of the day. In the evening, as she was about to leave him to Fredericks' ministrations, he said abruptly, "Isn't that masquerade thing of Georgiana's the day after tomorrow?"

"Yes. But I shall not go."

He eyed her smoldering profile resentfully. "Don't stay here on my account! Gran will be very pleased to bear me company, I've no doubt. I have no wish to come between you and your pleasures."

She turned away so that he could not see her face, but he knew from her rigid stance that she was weeping and cursed himself savagely.

"Oh, *queridisima*, forgive me! Come here, do . . . indeed I am a brute . . . a boorish monster to treat you so ill!"

With a great sob, she turned and flung herself upon him. "No, no, *mi esposo*! It is I who am bad! I scold you and scold you . . ."

"A regular little pepperpot!" he agreed unsteadily, his hand moving in her hair.

"It is only that I worry for you. . . ."

"I know, *alma mía*! And I do not deserve you!" He raised her face, wiped away the tears, and kissed her gently, and then with more passion. "You *must* go to Chiswick tomorrow. I want you to go. You know how you have been looking forward to it."

"But without you there, it will not be the same."

"Nevertheless, you will go. I insist. It will be good for you." He grimaced and said dryly, "I am sure Staveley will be happy to stand in my shoes."

She looked at him quickly. "You do not mind?"

"Mind? Of course I mind! I wish to God it were

me! But I owe him something, I suppose. I will survive the two days without you."

Pilar felt very odd wearing her old gypsy clothes. It was hard to know why she had even kept them; at first it had been a desire to cling to old ties, old values, and afterward they had lain forgotten at the back of the closet. When Georgiana had suggested the masquerade, she had remembered and sent down to Ashenden for them.

But now, she wished she had not. She had put on a little weight and the waistband of the black skirt was tight, constricting her; she was suddenly filled with a curious sense of foreboding, as though the tightness concealed bonds which were imprisoning her, drawing her inexorably back through time.

The elegant white and gold bedchamber at Chiswick seemed unreal; the music, wafting up through the open windows from terraces where hundreds of lanterns were strung out among the trees, grew faint as her heightened imagination ran riot: How awful to lose Theo, perhaps forever. . . .

Panic held her in a helpless grip. Georgiana knocked and came in; Pilar sank onto the bed with a sigh, loosened the lacings on the waistband, and at once the feeling left her.

"My love! Are you all right?"

"Yes," said Pilar faintly. "For one moment I had the strangest feeling. . . ."

Georgiana's beautiful blue eyes widened appreciatively. "My dear, you look quite distractingly lovely—such a pretty headdress. What a pity Theo can't be here. Mind you, we are like to be missing half our menfolk later. Charles is calling a meeting to see can anything be done to stop George Gordon . . . he really is making quite a nuisance of himself! Most disobliging of him to spoil my masquerade! But our Prince Florizel is here with his Perdita!"

Her voice dropped conspiratorially. "Rumor has it that his passion is cooling somewhat . . . of course, she is shockingly expensive! That house he bought for her near you in Berkeley Square is costing him a fortune!" And with another of her quicksilver changes of mood, "Do you like my costume?"

In her right hand she held a silver hunting spear, and as she spun around for Pilar's inspection the layers of gauze bound with cords about her magnificent figure clung, revealing more than Pilar could think seemly.

"Diana—goddess of the moon—virgin huntress and patroness of chastity!" Georgiana's eyes brimmed with amusement. "Do you have your mask? We can go down together." And ever restive, she held out a hand.

Three hours later the festivities were in full cry; the approach of midnight was heralded by a frenzied increase of hilarity; females in assorted disguises ran shrieking into the shrubberies hotly pursued by gentlemen eager to anticipate the moment of unmasking.

Pilar stood a little to one side, forgotten for the moment. Hers was by no means the only gypsy dress; she had counted at least six others; it occurred to her that Georgiana, in a quixotic mood, may have so arranged it to cause confusion. She wished that she had not allowed the Duchess to persuade her to dance.

"Just before midnight, my love—you will do it, won't you? Like you did at Charlie Rackam's? Those who saw you have talked of nothing else! I declare I shall give you no peace until you say yes!"

Pilar's memories of that night were still painful, but all her objections were overruled and without Theo's support her sensibilities were laughingly dismissed.

A group of gentlemen came through the open doors onto the terrace, engrossed in animated discussion. Mr. Fox was there, and young Lord Duncannon, Lord Ardwicke, Mr. Sheridan, and several others known to her only by sight.

By the time a chord of music was struck, reluctance had given way to a mood of fatalism. Mr. Staveley came up behind her. "You are going through with it, then?" His eyes glittered behind the mask, but she couldn't divine his expression.

"Why not?" she returned recklessly. "It is what everyone seems to want!"

Somehow, somewhere, Georgiana had found herself a genuine gypsy fiddler, and Pilar's blood quickened to the call of the sobbing rhythm with all the old abandon. As the final note died and she sank to the floor, the French clock in the salon chimed the first notes of midnight. The sound became drowned in a storm of cheers, bravos, and shouts of "Unmask!"

Laughing, still gasping for breath, Pilar tore off her mask with the rest, and as eager hands lifted her, she looked up—to find Lord Ardwicke staring at her in horror. Before she had a chance to speak, he had turned on his heel and walked away. While people surged around her, laughing and talking, she stood, the excitement draining away, his obvious disgust making her feel suddenly cheap.

As soon as she was able, she escaped and went in search of him.

"Lord Ardwicke?" said Georgiana. "No. I haven't seen him. Oh, but I shouldn't worry too much. He was probably preoccupied . . . all this talk of riots and revolution! And then the poor man has family problems—his wife, you know, is not at all strong! In fact, he may possibly have gone home—he lives not above five miles north of here."

Pilar was still troubled when Mr. Staveley found her. She related what had happened and her misery was apparent.

Mr. Staveley heard her out to the end and then said softly, "Well, well! So brother Harry has come to his reckoning at last! It's taken him long enough in all conscience!"

Something in his voice frightened her. "I do not understand you."

"No," he said. "But I believe the time has come for plain speaking." He took her arm and walked her purposefully through the now crowded salon and across the hall to a small, deserted parlor. To struggle would have drawn even more attention.

"This will serve," he ushered her inside and shut the door.

Pilar wrenched her arm free. "Are you quite mad, to bring me in here? Everyone has seen us!"

"Sit down, Pilar."

This curt familiarity, the curious emphasis he laid on her name, was something new. And the gray eyes were flint hard, appraising her. Her breath came suffocatingly fast.

"Thank you, but I shall not be staying. What is this plain speaking you must make with me?"

"As you will," he said abruptly. "You found my brother's behavior odd?" He reached into a small pocket in his waistcoat and laid something in the palm of her hand. "There you have the explanation."

She stared. "Oh! But this is my medallion!"

"No, my dear," he said softly. "That is *my* medallion." Mr. Staveley watched the wild color flood her face. "There were two, you see—one for me and one for Harry, my precious, highly respected brother Harry!"

Pilar heard the words, but her mind refused to accept what they were telling her. Mr. Staveley hated his brother . . . he was making the whole thing up, but she would not be so used!

"I do not believe you," she said. "There must be many such trinkets . . ."

He shook his head, almost pityingly. "Not so. Observe the originality of design?" He picked up the medallion and held it under her nose. "Our family crest. My father had them cast when we were children." He let the words sink in. "So you see, my dear, we are kin, you and I . . . you are Harry's daughter, his legitimate daughter, as I believe, and any day now I hope to prove it."

"No!" It was half cry, half groan. Her head moved angrily. "No. I will *not* believe it!" Before he could stop her, she was out of the door and running up the stairs.

15

Lord Ardwicke's villa was set back from the road along a winding lane shady with majestic elm trees, its rear gardens sloping invitingly down toward the river. The house was modest by comparison with Chiswick, but prettily proportioned. The cool, flower-filled hall had a homeliness which disconcerted Pilar but in no way swayed her from her purpose.

Her heart had been hardening throughout hot, sleepless hours of tossing and turning. She had liked the Earl so well! But her vigorous rejection of Mr. Staveley's cruel disclosures gradually crumbled as the insidious worm of logic made the impossible seem entirely probable until, in the end, she could no longer blind herself to the truth.

From then on, she had but to nurse her anger until she might face Lord Ardwicke, charge him with his infamy! She could scarcely wait for morning! If only she might make her departure without having to meet Mr. Staveley again. Amy was dispatched to discover if he was yet risen and returned with the slightly disconcerting news that Mr. Staveley had already breakfasted and gone.

It remained only for Pilar to order her coach and to pen a letter to Georgiana in the careful rounded hand so painstakingly taught her by Adam, blaming her departure on Theo's health . . . and a desire to return to his side with all speed. As a sudden wave of nausea swept over her, she remembered the baby and felt an overwhelming need for the reassurance of Theo's love. . . .

The pleasant, smiling footman who had taken her card had now returned with Lord Ardwicke's butler, who ushered her in an almost fatherly fashion up the gracefully curving staircase. She stood at the open door of the bright, chintz-hung salon, bolstering up her resolution with the force of her grievance, and finally entered with a swish of skirts to be further disconcerted at finding not Lord Ardwicke at all, but a fair, fragile-looking lady with a sweet, diffident smile, who reclined upon a chaise longue, her legs covered by a rug—and nearby, two girls, replicas of her.

The lady extended a hand. "Lady Gilmore . . . you are very welcome. Forgive me for presuming . . . you asked for my husband, I know, and he will be here directly. Benson has gone to find him. We have so few visitors." It was wistfully said. "Forgive me for not rising—a weakness in my back makes me quite stupidly slow and clumsy to move . . ."

"Alice! Benson says . . ." The door was thrown open and Pilar turned in sudden confusion to face the grave, courteous, and disconcertingly youthful man who was her father. This was not in the least how she had planned the confrontation. Their eyes met—and the full admission of his guilt lay in the swift, anguished glance he directed toward his wife and family and then back to her, as though willing her—to do what? To be merciful? Had he shown her mother mercy?

"Lady Gilmore," he said quietly, so quietly that

only she heard the catch of his breath. "May I present my wife and my daughters. Francine, Jane, make your curtsies to Lady Gilmore." The girls, not long out of the schoolroom, bobbed enthusiastically, eyeing Pilar's modish traveling dress with frank curiosity and envy. "Our son, James, is at present away at school," he added, the strain telling in his voice.

Pilar's emotions were undergoing a series of distressing fluctuations. These people had no place in her reckoning! They were charming people—unassuming—an obviously devoted family. The whole of this house exuded happiness, and she had come here determined to wreak her vengeance! Her lips made polite conversation while her head and heart fought desperately for supremacy.

"Will you take tea, Lady Gilmore?" Prompted by her mother, Francine asked the question with a grave, blushing shyness which moved Pilar more than she could wish.

"Oh, no! Thank you, but I must not . . . my husband . . . I would not have come, only that there was something . . . I had to . . ." Oh, *Madre*! This was dreadful.

Lord Ardwicke came to her rescue. "My dear Alice, I believe that Lady Gilmore is in something of a dilemma—a pressing matter of business. Will you think us very rude if we retire to my study?"

In the small room, comfortably appointed with much oak paneling, the Earl watched his newfound daughter walk to the window and stand—a stiff, unyielding figure staring blindly out toward the river. Compassion outweighed all other emotions and he found that nothing in his diplomatic life had equipped him for such a situation. "My dear child . . ." he began, and trailed off.

"All these years I have hated you, did you know?" she blurted out, the painful tears choking her. "It is very easy to hate someone you have never met. But you are not as I thought. . . ."

"Whereas you are exactly like your mother!" he said with a soft intensity. "I must have been blind not to have seen it from the first. Small wonder that I felt so at ease in your company! Yet, when the rumors reached my ears, I refused to lend them credence—they stirred memories I was ashamed to recall!" His voice trembled slightly. "And then, last night, it was as if the years between had never been; Rosanne looked out at me from your eyes—and like a callow youth I turned tail and ran!"

Into the silence that followed, Pilar said harshly, "It was a night for revelations, it seems. Your true daughter, Mr. Staveley inferred, and not a bastard child at all! He said he would prove it." She turned and met his eyes accusingly. The anguish she saw there almost broke her heart. But she must not feel sorry for him.

"My brother has been busy, indeed!"

"*Then it is true!*" she whispered, feeling none of the elation the knowledge should have brought her. "And if I had not found out . . . would you have told me?"

He passed a hand wearily across his face. "I don't know. I have spent the night in a torment of indecision."

"Because you were in danger of betrayal!"

"No! Oh, can you not try to understand, child? Until now, I had not dreamed of your existence! My dilemma was in deciding how far the truth would serve you. Will you be any happier, do you think, for knowing it?"

"It was never happiness that I craved!" Pilar

cried passionately. "It was to be revenged upon you for my mother's heartbreak, and for what you made of me!"

He flinched. "Then you have only to be patient for a little longer, my dear, and Francis will achieve your ambition for you!" There was a wealth of bitterness in the words. "He has envied my position for so long! He must be overjoyed to have it within his power at last to bring me down."

"And is that any more than you deserve? When you have lived a lie for so long!" It was a last, half-hearted attempt to dredge up all the hatred nurtured over the years—and she immediately wished the words unsaid. He turned away from her to sit in a chair near the fireplace, his head in his hands. Pilar followed him swiftly and sank to her knees beside him, tugging at his arm.

"No, no! I should not have spoken so! My tongue should be cut out for its wickedness! Always Theo is rebuking me for it! Ah, senor—I do not really wish you so ill. Let the past remain buried! I no longer care!"

"If only that were possible!" The Earl pulled himself together and raised a haggard face in a bleak smile. "You are more gracious than I deserve!"

He lifted her hand to his lips and then retained it, kneading it almost absently in his own as he spoke. "But Francis will pursue this thing to the end. It is a chance he must scarce have dreamed of—can you see him letting it slip?"

"With proof, he can force me to disinherit James—acknowledge himself as my lawful heir. As such, his prospects would be vastly improved—and to a man who gambles as recklessly as Francis, that would be no mean advantage!" A look of pain crossed the gentle face. "Yet even that would not weigh with him as much as the thought of humbling me."

"Does he hate you so much?"

"I believe so. God knows why, except that, being so much the elder, my father always made more of me." He shrugged. "Poor Francis! By the time he had grown to manhood my father was dead and I was already possessed of a son and heir. He was obliged to make do with a younger son's portion, a growing pile of debts, and few prospects; forced to come cap in hand to me when his creditors grew too pressing."

"He did not have to live so," protested Pilar. "He could have made a useful life, as you have done."

"Ah, but I always had a flair for languages, which is how I came by the post of junior secretary to Lord Bristol in Madrid—and thus met your mother."

Pilar's breath caught sharply; instinctively she withdrew her hand and then, seeing her father's expression, gave it back to him.

"Will you tell me how it was? I would like to understand!"

He looked at her, but she thought it was another face he saw. "I was nineteen, a little wild—at that age one is careless of reputation." He smiled faintly, remembering. "I went out one night with a crowd of other, equally light-minded young men to explore some of the less salubrious night spots. In one of them I found Rosanne. She was very young and very, very beautiful—and quite plainly terrified of the oaf who accompanied her.

"With all the arrogance of youth, I dispatched him into the night and returned to a shy gratitude which did nothing to disguise her continuing terror. The man was important, it seemed—her parents would be angry. By the time I had reassured her, we were already head over ears in love! We continued to meet secretly, and then one night she didn't arrive!"

He was gripping Pilar's hand uncomfortably hard without being aware of it.

"I waited in an agony and when she came the following night, she had quite obviously been badly beaten up. Her father had heard talk of a man—a *Gorgio*—worse, an English *Gorgio*. There was little love for the English at that time—we were on the verge of war."

Lord Ardwicke looked steadily at his daughter. "I did the only thing I could do—we were married secretly by a friendly padre, and I installed Rosanne in rooms well out of reach of her people. As God is my judge, child—at that moment I had every intention of acknowledging her as my wife. But she was painfully shy, ill at ease, needed time to adjust, and I allowed myself to be persuaded.

"And then everything went wrong at once—I went down with some kind of fever, and while I lay in a delirium, the Embassy was ordered home and our Government declared war on Spain. By the time I regained my senses, I was back home in Surrey, appallingly weak and at first convinced that the whole thing had been a dream. I let the days slip by; the family cosseted me, and Alice, who was the daughter of a near neighbor, became a frequent visitor. . . ."

Pilar's foot had gone to sleep, but she endured the discomfort for fear of breaking the flow of his narrative.

"For what happened next I can only plead in

mitigation some lingering weakness. A marriage was suggested between Alice and myself. We had grown fond of one another and, but for the memory of Rosanne I would not have hesitated. As it was, I wrestled with my conscience, afraid to tell my father what I had done—and finally, to my shame, I convinced myself that Rosanne would long since have given me up for lost and resumed her old life." His sigh seemed to come from deep inside him. "It was an unforgivable decision, for once made, it became relatively easy to put it to the back of my mind."

Pilar thought of the broken shell of a woman she had known—silent and a little distraught—and for a moment the old bitterness returned.

"They would never have taken her back," she said bleakly. "It is not the gypsy way. She took to the road—living from day to day, caring for me well enough, but her spirit had died with her hope. She never spoke of you by name, only muttering sometimes of '*mi esposo*.' But when she had grown ill and frail she brought me to England; I believe she meant to seek you out in order to provide for me. But she was not equal to such a journey."

She gave him a brief, but illuminating account of her life before Theo came and when it was done he said harshly, "Then, God knows, you have every right to hate me . . . to demand whatever restitution you may see fit. The least I can do is to acknowledge you as my daughter. . . ."

Pilar's mind flew swiftly to the happy family group, visualizing the effect such a pronouncement would have. "You must not! There is no need. My mother is at rest and I am content with Theo, who loves me as I am! To reveal what is past would be cruel! Only consider your poor wife. . . ."

The Earl's face took on a haunted look. "Do you think I have not racked my brain? How do I reconcile Alice to the fact that our seventeen years together have been a travesty of all she holds most sacred? And what of the girls—and James? How do I tell my son that he is not Viscount Staveley, but a bastard?"

"You must not! There is no need."

He groaned. "My dear, you are forgetting Francis."

"Your brother must be made to see . . ."

"Why? Is he not entitled to his pound of flesh? He is, after all, the rightful heir."

"How can you say this?" Pilar demanded hotly. "When he would ruin you!"

Her father smiled wryly at her forceful denunciation. "Perhaps the knowledge of my own guilt puts me for once in sympathy with him. But I'd give a monkey to know what set him off."

"He saw my medallion," Pilar confessed. "The one you gave to my mother. It bears your crest."

"Ah!"

"I thought nothing of it at the time, but he remarked on it at our very first meeting."

"It would be sufficient to spur him into action," said the Earl ruefully. "He would dig patiently until he uncovered the whole sordid story. No doubt the instigation of the gossip may also be laid at his door."

"Oh, no!" Pilar explained about Mrs. Verney.

"Then he could only have laughed at his good fortune!"

"Perhaps he won't find his proof," she said, to be comforting.

This time he raised a soft laugh and drew her into the curve of his arm. "Oh, my dear! Come what may, I am glad to have you for my daughter!"

"*Muy bien!* I, too, am content that you are my father," she sighed, and leaned her head half-shyly against his shoulder. "It is a very comfortable thing to have a father. Do you know?"

He dropped a kiss on her hair and they sat for some moments in a companionable silence.

"Well," he said. "We shall just have to be patient and await Francis's next move. It is always possible that he might have traced the tiny church where your mother and I were married, though I doubt his resources would stretch to such a search. The only other record that exists, to my knowledge, is a small certificate of marriage which I placed for Rosanne's safekeeping in a rather uncommon snuff box of mine. If only she had made use of it!"

He was astonished when Pilar leaped to her feet.

"A gold box—with little panels of enamel?"

He sat forward, suddenly animated. "You have it?"

"Yes. But I don't understand. There was nothing . . ."

"Did Francis know you had it?" he pressed her urgently.

Pilar stared at him, uncomprehending at first. "He saw it once," she said slowly. "When we were at Ashenden. He wished me to sell it to him."

"You did not . . .?"

"No! I would never part from it! But, I don't understand . . ."

"The box has a false bottom! There is a spring most ingeniously concealed behind one of the enamel motifs. It so intrigued me when I first acquired it, I showed it to Francis, who was then but a boy . . ."

"And he would remember! But how did he know the marriage lines were hidden there?"

"He didn't. But Francis is a gambler, remember. It is precisely where he would conceal something he wished to keep safe."

"Then the matter is simple, dear senor," said Pilar, taking his hand. "You shall have the box the moment I am able to restore it to you, and you may destroy your evidence."

Pilar found the journey home tedious in the extreme. The coach was unbelievably stuffy and she wished very much to arrive—to share with Theo the extraordinary turn her life had taken. He would perhaps know how to prevent Francis Staveley from making trouble for Lord Ardwicke. She still found difficulty in thinking of him as her father.

Reaching Berkeley Square, she ran quickly up the stairs, throwing her hat to Amy and calling cheerfully to Meecham, who observed, not for the first time, how the whole house came alive when his young mistress was present.

Lady Penridding was nodding comfortably in her favorite chair in the sunny drawing room, but roused sufficiently to inquire whether the masquerade had been a success.

So much had happened since, that Pilar had almost forgotten the masquerade, but she promised to return when she had seen Theo, to tell her all about it.

Before seeing Theo she went on an impulse to her own room to find the snuff box. It was gone! At first she refused to believe; she tipped one drawer after another onto the floor, searching frantically among the tumbled contents while Amy looked on in astonishment.

"Why, milady! Whatever are you in such a taking about?"

Pilar sat back on her heels at last amid the disarray, filled with angry despair. So that was why Francis had left Chiswick with such haste! Oh, he was clever, that one! It never occurred to her for one moment to doubt his guilt; easy enough, after all, to cajole some poor, half-witted servant girl or bribe an underpaid footman with a promise of gold! The how was unimportant beside the much more vexing question of why? What use would he make of his advantage—and, more crucially, how could he be stopped?

Pilar half heard Amy as she repeated her entreaty. "I am sorry," she said, staring at the disorder around her. "I wanted my enameled box, but it is not here."

"Oh! And it was that pretty! Mayhap you've left it in a pocket. I'll turn the closets out."

"If you wish," her mistress said without interest. "You will not find it, I think."

She straightened up and went with slightly lagging step into Theo's room, and found him just put back to bed by Fredericks and striving to mask his weariness behind the ardor of his welcome.

"May I say how pleased we are to see you back, ma'am, said Fredericks, adding with a certain severity, "You will find his lordship a little tired, having succumbed to the oppressiveness of the day."

"The devil, I have! You make me sound like a maiden aunt with the vapors! The only thing I find oppressive around here is a crabby old fool who fusses worse than my wife and ain't half so pretty!"

"Just as you say, sir." The insult was received by the valet with astonishing mildness, it being a sure sign of his lordship's continuing improvement. He exchanged a comprehensive look with Lady Gilmore as he left the room, observing as he did so that she seemed to have derived little benefit from her excursion.

Theo privately thought so, too, as she sat beside him on the bed, scolding him.

"Never mind me, *querida*. How was Georgiana's party?"

Pilar, her emotions balanced on a fine edge, abandoned all she had meant to pour out to him.

"I am so happy to be with you again!" she gulped, and burst into tears.

Theo held her close, wondering what had gone wrong. Had Georgiana's stupid prank misfired? "I should never have agreed to your going without me!" he said forcefully. "It was madness!"

"Oh, no!" Pilar reassured him. "I am being very silly, *mi esposo*, only because I have missed you so!" Her kiss demonstrated to him how much. Tomorrow she would confide in him—when he was rested. She sat back with a determined sniff. "Have you been taking your draught as you promised?"

"Small chance of my forgetting with that old wet nurse, Fredericks, looming over the sickroom."

Her giggle bubbled up as a kind of release. "Poor man! You are not kind to him. Sometimes he looks as though he will cry!"

"Don't you believe it! My insults are the breath of life to him. How else could he convince himself of his own superiority?"

This time her laugh was spontaneous.

"That's much better," he said. "I think you had better not go away and leave me again, my love. It puts circles under your eyes and makes me confoundedly restless. Everyone is so civil—I find myself ridiculously at a loss without you to scold and throw pots at my head!"

"I do not . . ."

"Of course you do not!" he soothed, and pulled her back into the circle of his arm. "Tell me, how would you feel about going to Ashenden?"

"Oh, yes."

"Gran suggested it yesterday, and I confess I would welcome the change. I'm heartily sick of this hothouse and the eternal stream of visitors—and if I have to listen to any more about Lord George Gordon and the Roman Catholic peers, I shall have a relapse! That old bore, Horry Walpole, was here this morning going on about it—and quizzing me about you!" Theo stifled a yawn. "Much good it did him. . . ."

Pilar slid from the bed and insisted that he should not say another word. His eyes were already closing as she left. Wanting only to go to her room and think, she nevertheless went down to the drawing room and gave Lady Penridding a deliberately light-hearted account of the party.

"Has Theo mentioned going to Ashenden?"

"Yes. And it would be the very best thing for him," Pilar agreed.

"For you both, I shouldn't wonder," said the old lady shrewdly. "Give you a little time to yourselves. No, I'll not come with you," she added, seeing Pilar's surprise. "Time I returned to Theo's grandfather—though I doubt he's even noted my absence! Gertrude's welcome to stay on here, if she's a mind. I've more than done my duty by her, and if she don't bring Lord Montague up to scratch any day now, she's not the woman I take her for!

Whether she can induce Letty to have him, though, I make leave to doubt! The child's got more spunk than I thought, and she's head over ears in love with young Beaumont. . . . Ah, well, they may fight it out without me. Like Theo, I'd welcome a little peace and quiet."

By the following morning Pilar was quite certain in her mind what she must do. To tell Theo now would not answer; he might not understand her own feelings in the matter, and suppose he were to insist on calling Francis Staveley out—or even her father! No, she could not take such a chance!

Instead, she would go to Francis Staveley herself—appeal to him to do nothing rash, to at least meet with his brother and work out a solution that would do the least hurt to Lord Ardwicke's family. Pilar could not believe him so wicked that he would pillory innocent people—his own kin—to serve his ambition. It needed only someone to explain matters to him.

16

Pilar had visited Mr. Staveley's rooms in Half Moon Street only once, for a card party, but found her way with surprising ease. There were more people about than she had expected—a noisy crowd, for the most part, who pushed past her without ceremony. She was glad she had dressed as incomspicuously as possible, and instinctively drew the light shawl closer about her face. One of the first precepts instilled into her by Theo had been that a lady never went unaccompanied into the street, but for the moment far older instincts held sway and she merged into the throng without fear.

She did feel a certain guilt about the deceptions she had practiced in order to slip out of the house unnoticed, but they were quickly pushed to the back of her mind.

The surly manservant who answered her knocking showed little disposition to be helpful.

"Master's not at home," he muttered.

"Oh." Quite stupidly, this possibility had never occurred to her. She felt a little spurt of anger that all her planning had been for nothing. "Will he return soon, do you think?"

"Couldn't say. He don't acquaint me of his comings and goings." The man's tone indicated only too plainly his opinion of females who called at a gentleman's rooms uninvited.

Pilar wasn't sure what to do. To leave with nothing accomplished seemed futile. She glanced uneasily about her—it would not do to be recognized. A man ran past, almost knocking her down.

"I will step inside and wait. The matter is of *considerable* importance!" She rolled the phrase out impressively—grudgingly the manservant opened the door wider and she stepped into the hall.

"*Gracias.*"

On the opposite side of the hall a door stood open; she could just see a desk. An idea—bold—impossible—unforgivable if she were discovered—came to her. The man was chewing, eyeing her in a manner bordering on insolence.

"Now! You may perhaps be able to assist me." Her most autocratic voice had some effect. "My husband visited Mr. Staveley recently and he left behind his snuff box. It was a very individual piece—in gold, with panels of enamel. Have you seen such a box?"

"No."

"Then you will oblige me by looking for it. It is imperative that the box is found!"

Pilar prayed that the servant would be too stupid—or too in awe of her—to wonder why a lady would come on her husband's errands. After a moment's hesitation the man shuffled off up the stairs, grumbling to himself, and as he disappeared she sped lightly across the hall, with no idea of what she was hoping for—a miracle, perhaps?

The room was a kind of study, smelling faintly of leather; a small, heavily latticed window let in brilliant points of sunlight to wink over a table scattered with papers, and opposite the door a rosewood writing bureau, closed but with the key left carelessly in the lock. It would be a matter of moments only to look inside!

At first her search seemed hopeless, but to one side there were three small drawers and in the second of these her search was rewarded. She opened the snuff box; her own marriage lines were still there and she took them and stuffed them hastily down the front of her dress. Her breath was coming so fast now that she felt dizzy! What had Lord Ardwicke said about the panels? Her fingers grew slippery with perspiration and shook as she tugged and pulled. One after after another she tried, and at last, when she had given up hope, there was a small click and a panel swiveled sideways revealing a tiny, delicately fashioned lever beneath. The lightest of touches and with a faint whirring sound the base of the box flew open. It was empty! Her disappointment was so intense, she cried aloud.

"Is this what you are seeking?" asked Francis Staveley. He closed the door with ominous quiet and walked toward her, his coat skirts swishing audibly in the silence. Between finger and thumb he dangled a folded, yellowing paper enticingly. His voice was soft, but his eyes were flint-hard.

"Did you suppose I would be so foolish as to leave such a precious document unguarded after all the trouble I have taken to acquire it?"

Foolish? No, she had been the fool—fool to come in here in the first place—fool to think stealing so easy—fool, most of all, when she had found what she sought, to stay and be found out!

She looked back at him proudly. "Though you will not believe me, I did not come to steal from you."

His eyes traveled over his vandalized desk, and his brows lifted in disbelief.

"It is true!" Pilar insisted, coloring. "But the door stood open . . . and . . . it happened . . . an impulse."

"And now the door is shut—and I must decide what I am to do with you."

"Do with me?" she echoed faintly.

"Only consider, my dear—how embarrassing for your husband if I call a constable and have you taken up for stealing?"

She drew a sharp breath and laughed nervously. "You are making fun with me, I think? We are related, you and I."

"So we are."

"And that is why I came," she hurried on. "To talk with you, to beg you not to turn against your brother in a way which will hurt so many innocent people!"

"How touching!" he drawled. And then more harshly, "Is not what Harry did as bad?"

"Perhaps, but . . ."

"My God!" he exclaimed. "How does he do it? He has even got around you!"

"No, but I can see how it happened, all those years ago . . ."

"And you are sorry for him! You see? He has a smooth tongue and charming manners. He is universally acclaimed as a fine fellow—kind to his wife and children—intelligent, equable—a godsend to governments in need of a mediator!" He came closer and took Pilar's chin urgently in his fingers, and she met the full force of his bitterness. Its intensity scared her.

"And what do they say of Francis? Oh, he's well enough, I suppose, but a gambler, a bit unsteady, perhaps—and of course, not a patch on his brother!" His fingers bit hard. "Well, I may be all those things, but by God, I'm the more honest—at least I haven't lived in a state of bigamy for the last seventeen years!"

Madre de Dios! He was indeed a little mad and would need careful handling. Pilar put up a hand to cover the one imprisoning her chin, and felt his fingers tighten as he moved to jerk it away.

"I know how you must feel—I, too, have been bitter. But you do yourself too little justice, for you also are kind, as I can testify. But for you, my Theo might now be dead."

To her astonishment he seemed amused and the full horror slowly dawned. "It was you who shot Theo!" she whispered. "That is why you were so conveniently on hand. But why? What could you hope to achieve by killing Theo?"

"My dear girl, had I wished to kill your husband he would now be dead. I don't make mistakes of that kind!"

"Then I don't understand. . . ."

"It is really quite simple. I wanted him out of the way before the masquerade. I had discovered what Georgiana was planning I knew also Harry was to be there and that the sight of you in that gypsy dress, looking, I am sure, the image of your mother, could well precipitate a violent reaction. My brother has been sweating under the threat of those rumors. Had you not noticed how he was beginning to avoid you?"

From somewhere came a sound of crashing glass. Staveley frowned distastefully and continued, "Since Mrs. Verney's departure seems to have brought about a most boring display of marital harmony between you and Theo, I was forced to consider what sort of a stand he might take in the event of trouble. Rather than risk his spoiling sport, I decided to render him . . . temporarily inactive."

Pilar could hardly believe what she was hearing. "But that is monstrous! And afterward you brought me flowers! Showed me such concern!"

"But I *was* concerned! I would have been most distressed had Theo's wound proved fatal."

Contemptuous anger blazed in her eyes. "*And* you stole my box!"

"Ah, yes—the snuff box! Harry will have explained its hidden attractions? My curiosity was aroused when I saw it in your possession. The medallion had already led me to make certain inquiries, and here was a trinket much treasured by my brother, one he would not easily part with, unless of course there was good reason. I had meant to have it from you long since. I spent some time cultivating a certain little housemaid at Ashenden, and then quite suddenly you went away and I had to make new plans to acquire it." He shrugged. "But I am a patient man. Harry was in America— and when he returned there was already talk, which I was pleased to feed a little. The results were quite pleasing. No one, I find, is quite as guilt-ridden as a virtuous man who has strayed. Don't you agree?"

Pilar remembered Lord Ardwicke's agony of conscience and her anger against Francis grew until it consumed her. . . . The room was stifling . . . her head seemed as if it must surely burst. . . .

"I am leaving," she gasped. "I cannot stay another moment in this place with you!"

He continued to bar her path. "I can't allow you to go—not quite yet. No, truly," he insisted as she moved violently in protest. "There is a mob loose on the streets. Did you not hear the glass breaking a moment ago? Gordon has been preaching his anti-Popery campaign down in the East End again and has stirred up rather more hatred than he can contain. Who can tell how far it will spread?"

"I do not care! I would prefer the mob ten times over to your company!" She spat the words at him.

"Nevertheless, you will stay," he said, "until I can send for your father to escort you safe home."

"No! I will not be used as a weapon in your quarrels!"

He stood so close that Pilar's back was pressed uncomfortably against the bureau. If only she might reach her knife, she would kill him! She put a steadying hand on the desk—and as though in answer to her thoughts her fingers closed on something. She glanced down; it was indeed a knife of kinds, not so good as her own, but adequate.

She raised it, grim with purpose. "Now. You will let me go!"

Instinctively, Mr. Staveley had stepped back a pace. Now he smiled sardonically. "Or what, my dear? Would you kill me?" He opened his arms invitingly. "Come along, then. I'm sure you know the way of it. A swift upward thrust—about here, I should say."

Pilar couldn't do it—couldn't move; she looked despairingly at the knife and knew herself beaten. Mr. Staveley knew it, too. He reached across and twisted her wrist, and the weapon dropped harmlessly back on the desk.

"Poor Pilar! They have civilized you too well, it seems!"

She glared at him, nursing the bruised wrist.

"And now," he said softly, "shall we go up to my salon to wait for Harry?"

A feeling of unease hung like a pall over Penridding House. It was not until Theo, feeling very much improved, decided to dine downstairs and found his grandmother alone in the drawing room that he discovered Pilar's absence. Letty and her mother had gone to luncheon at the Montagues. Meecham, when appealed to, ascertained that Lady Gilmore had not taken one of the carriages, ". . . but it is possible that she took a chair, ma'am," he added without conviction.

Dinner was put back and by the time Meecham came again to say that Amy was very agitated and asking for her ladyship, nerves were becoming stretched. Lord Gilmore's presence seemed to put Amy in even more of a quake.

"Eh, I'm that worried, m'lord . . . ma'am. Her ladyship's been gone over three hours, I reckon . . ."

"Alone?" snapped Theo.

"Seemingly so, m'lord, though it weren't my fault!" Indignation momentarily overcame her tears. "She sent me out on an errand and when I got back she were gone. Well, I didn't think a owt about it for a start, her being of a somewhat impulsive turn of mind, but now . . . and what with all those dreadful things going on, not a mile nor more away . . ."

"Lady Gilmore is probably safe at Devonshire House," Lady Penridding said bracingly. "Meecham, have a message taken around there at once."

"With respect, ma'am," said Meecham, looking unhappy, "her Grace arrived, not fifteen minutes since, at Lord Claremont's residence—in quite a taking she was, I am told, fearing that Devonshire House was no longer safe from the mob."

"Mercy on us! Have matters got so badly out of hand?" Her Ladyship, striving for her grandson's sake to hide her dismay, marveled, not for the first time, how swiftly news traveled below stairs. "Well then, Pilar must be elsewhere—at the Beaumont's perhaps?"

Amy let out a doleful sniff.

"For heaven's sake, girl!" Worry drove Theo to unnecessary sharpness. "Your mistress is well able to take care of herself. You should know that."

"That's as may be, m'lord, but . . ." Amy's manner hovered between acute embarrassment and a determination to do her duty or perish in the attempt. She looked despairingly at Lady Penridding as though for help. "It's not my way to speak out of turn, ma'am, as well you know, and in the ordinary way my lips would stay sealed, no matter what . . ."

"Amy!" Theo's exasperation was mounting. "If you've something pertinent to say, for God's sake, say it!"

His grandmother frowned at him and beckoned the girl closer, her manner surprisingly gentle. "What is it that troubles you, child?"

Amy took a deep breath. "Well, for a start, something happened at the party . . . I don't know what, but it fair upset her. And besides that . . . well, she's been as sick as a dog these past few mornings!" She blurted it out, blushing furiously.

"Ah!"

"You'll not let on I've blabbed? I'd not have her think. . . ."

Theo looked from one to the other. "Will one of you kindly talk sense?"

"What Amy is saying, my dear," said the old lady slowly, "is that Pilar is most likely going to have a child."

His joy turned instantly to apprehension. "And

she's out there alone somewhere?" He stood up. "I must find her."

"Sit down, Theo! Don't be a fool!" Lady Penridding nodded dismissal to Amy, who scurried out. "You are in no state to do anything. We must stay calm." Two bright spots of color, brighter than her rouge, belied her words. "If only Adam were here!"

The door opened and Gertrude swept in, trailing a defiant Letty. She was in a towering rage. She began without preamble. "Never have I been so humiliated! The ingratitude of one's children is a cross every mother must bear, but this is beyond everything!"

They stared at her distorted, puce-colored face as though in a daze.

"Of course," she paced the room, gesticulating with a tightly clutched handkerchief, "I know where the blame lies! From the day you married that creature, there has been nothing but trouble . . ."

"Gertrude!" snapped Lady Penridding.

"What the devil are you ranting on about?" asked Theo in a curiously tight voice.

Gertrude's bosom heaved. "Lord Montague offered for Letty today, and she has refused him—turned him down flat in favor of that nonentity, Beaumont . . ."

"Gervaise is not a nonentity!" cried Letty, incensed.

"May I remind you, Gertrude that the Beaumonts are friends of mine," said her ladyship coldly.

"Good for you, Letty," said Theo, holding out a hand to her. She burst into tears and rushed to him. "For your information, ma'am," he said over her head, "I thoroughly approve of Gervaise Beaumont. In fact, it was I and not my wife who encouraged the affair. And now, if you don't mind, we are rather preoccupied . . ."

"Oh, of course! I know I have never counted for anything in this house . . ."

"That is not true, Gertrude." Lady Penridding was sitting rigidly erect; she strove to make her voice calm. "But if we might defer discussion until later? We are very worried about Pilar . . ."

"I might have known! I quite see that my affairs are of no importance when compared with *Pilar!*" She flounced toward the door.

Lady Penridding could hardly bear the contained anguish in Theo's face.

"Pilar is missing," he said bleakly.

Letty cried out and for once even Gertrude's look of complacent martyrdom was shaken. As she turned, the door opened and Meecham came in.

"Lord Ardwicke is here, my lady. He would like a word with Lord Gilmore."

17

Lord Ardwicke's coach was constantly impeded on its way to Half Moon Street. Inside the coach the silence was somewhat constrained; neither man noticed what went on outside, each being fully preoccupied with his own thoughts.

Lord Ardwicke for his part was facing the disintegration of all that he held most dear; there was no longer any hope that his family might be spared; his disgrace would be theirs also, Francis would make sure of that!

Theo was turning over yet again Ardwicke's extraordinary confession, made in the privacy of the library at Penridding House not half an hour since, culminating as it did in the message, amounting almost to an ultimatum, that he had received from his brother.

"Are you telling me that Staveley holds my wife as some kind of hostage against your appearance?"

"So it would seem, Gilmore. I can't tell you how distressed I am."

"The hell with your distress, man! What are you going to do about it?"

"I mean to go to Half Moon Street at once, of course," said Lord Ardwicke stiffly. "I came here first to assure myself that Francis was not bluffing and to set your mind at ease as to Pilar's whereabouts. Francis will not harm her, I am sure!"

"Thank you!" said Theo with heavy irony. "You relieve my mind!" He thought about his volatile wife; she would not submit easily. Pray heaven she would not lose her temper!

"I shall come with you," he said decisively.

"My lord, are you yet strong enough?"

"I don't know what Pilar is to you, but she is my wife! Do you imagine for one moment that I will sit here calmly while she is in that man's hands?"

Lady Penridding's objections had been voiced more pungently. "You are mad, Theo! I am sure I don't know what all this is about, or why Lord Ardwicke comes to learn of Pilar's whereabouts. Is *he* not able to escort her home? To consider chasing off on some mad ploy when you are hardly back on your feet is unthinkable! Who knows what the streets will be like—Gertrude said their coach was almost overturned twice on the way home!"

Nothing she said, however, could turn Theo from his purpose. He kissed her quite gently, told her not to worry, and strode from the room. In the hall he took his loaded pistol from a silent, disapproving Fredericks.

"Cheer up, man," he said with a forced grin.

"At least permit me to accompany you, my lord?" pleaded the unhappy valet.

"No need!" said the Viscount.

When they arrived, he climbed stiffly down from the coach. The drift of smoke caught sharply in his nostrils, bringing all his senses fully into focus. For the first time he noticed the red glow in the sky.

"Good God!" he exclaimed. "Are they trying to burn down the whole city?"

"You may well ask," Lord Ardwicke replied grimly. "The rabble are quite out of control. Gordon will have a lot to answer for when this is over. The chapels of the Foreign Ambassadors are pillaged and destroyed . . . Newgate in flames . . . Bedford House sacked . . . and the night hardly begun! Most of the Catholic families are in peril—Charles has gone to help defend Rockingham's house against attack. Make no mistake, it will end with the King calling out the troops!"

In Mr. Staveley's salon at the rear of the house, Pilar, too, was looking out on the angry sky. She sat on a settle with her feet drawn up, motionless, remote. Several times Francis Staveley addressed her, but she gave no sign of hearing him and he finally shrugged and left her alone.

It was a curious sensation—like floating; from the casement windows, thrown wide, came distant sounds of violence, people shouting, but the sounds became muted as time slipped away. She was not Lady Gilmore, but Pilar, the unwanted little gypsy half-breed, standing before old Ursula truculently demanding *"But I want to know!"*

With astonishing clarity she heard again the quavering voice. "Sometimes, little *chavi*, it is better not to know what comes to us. . . ."

But with the tenacious obstinacy of the very young, Pilar had plagued the old woman until Ursula, whose face was as old as eternity and who had the seeer's eye, sighed, her voice taking on strange cadences as though she were in a trance.

"Listen, then, for your destiny lies far from the Romany. I see splendor, riches a'plenty . . . but also tragedy. Three men, there are . . . one dark, black-haired as any Romany, but a fine English *raior*, for all that. He would hold you safe, but there are two brothers, fair and well-favored. You stand between them—one hides a black heart, the other a secret he would carry to the grave. . . ."

Here, Ursula had fallen silent. shaking her head and muttering until Pilar, hopping excitedly, had urged her on.

"Fire!" The voice was suddenly clear again. "Violence—and death!"

Pilar the child, secure in the confidence of childhood, had reveled in the delicious prickles of fear along her spine, and when the old woman could be persuaded no more, had allowed her imagination to run riot until, sated with possibilities, she tired of the game and like a dream it faded from her mind.

But Pilar the woman, remembering the words so clearly after all that time, shivered, feeling again the prickle of fear. It was happening as Ursula had predicted—would tonight perhaps see an ending? Her hands moved instinctively to protect that new life, the seed of love already burgeoning within her. If she died, Theo would never know of his child. With her arms still locked across her body, she comforted her unborn baby with a gentle rocking motion that was as old as time, while the tears rolled soundlessly down her cheeks.

The opening of the door went unnoticed until a familiar voice called her name. She looked up and saw them ranged all three, as though summoned by the forces of her imagination—her father and Francis . . . and Theo.

"Theo!" She sprang up with a cry and rushed upon him. "*Mi esposo*, you are here! I thought perhaps I was never to see you again and I was miserable. Now I do not care what happens!"

Theo drew her close and over her head his eyes sought Staveley and there was murder in the look. "You are all right, *querida*? He hasn't harmed you?"

She stirred indignantly. "That one? Never!" The full impact of Theo's presence suddenly hit her, and she pulled away from him. "But you should not be here! How are you here?"

"I came with Ardwicke," he explained carefully. "To demand satisfaction of Staveley."

Francis Staveley, on seeing Theo, grew tight about the mouth.

"Don't be a fool, Gilmore. My quarrel is with Harry, not with you."

"Then you should have kept it that way. Instead, you had the effrontery to abduct my wife. That makes it my quarrel, too. We will settle it now."

"No!" Pilar cried. "*Madre de Dios!* You are crazy! Has he not almost killed you once, already?"

She regretted the words the moment they were out, but it was too late. Theo's eyes narrowed.

"So that was the way of it! I always thought that affair had a nasty smell. No matter—it makes me doubly keen to teach you a lesson!"

Pilar looked wildly from one to the other and then to her father, who had not spoken since he entered the room. "Oh, please! Can you not stop them? Theo is too weak!"

Lord Ardwicke seemed to come suddenly to life. He stepped forward with a firm tread. "I regret you must wait your turn, Gilmore. I am before you by a good many years. I had not realized until recently how much my brother hated me." He turned to Francis. "I have overlooked much because I knew that I had wronged you, but in this matter you have gone too far."

"Not half as far as I mean to go, my brother!" sneered Staveley. "This time I mean to ruin you, once and for all."

"Then I must stop you, if I can. Lord Gilmore— you will oblige me by taking Pilar home. My coachman will drive you and then return to me here. My brother and I will better settle our differences without an audience."

Pilar was torn. She very much wanted to get Theo home where he would be safe. He looked so pale. But to leave her father alone with Francis, who was young, ambitious, and ruthless, filled her with a quite irrational dread.

"You mean to fight!" she accused him, and he did not deny it.

"Only if Francis will not listen to reason . . ."

"Reason! I'll listen to no more of your preaching, Harry, if that's what you intend!"

"Then you will fight," said Pilar with finality. She looked anxiously at Theo. "We cannot walk away, can we?"

"Oh, for God's sake, get out!" snapped Staveley, at the end of his patience. "Your part in this is ended. You were never more than a pawn in a much bigger game."

"You admit that you have used Pilar?" demanded Theo harshly, wishing his arm did not ache so abominably.

"Yes—I used her. She was there just asking to be used! Anyway, you should be grateful to me, Gilmore! I intend to legalize your wife's birth. Her mother may have been gypsy trash, but . . ."

He got no further. Lord Ardwicke's blow caught him flush on the mouth. He went down like a log and lay dazed for a moment before staggering to his feet.

"I'll not take that from you, Harry," he muttered, and walked unsteadily to the other end of the room, returning with an exceptionally fine pair of dueling swords.

"Father's," he said, his tongue flicking away a smear of blood from his cut lip. "You remember? You very generously made me a present of them when he died . . . to compensate perhaps for the lack of affection he bore me when he was alive!"

"I remember," said Lord Ardwicke. "Are you fit to fight?"

"I cannot wait!" said Francis viciously, already stripping off his coat and rolling up his sleeves.

The daylight had almost gone; the glow of flames against the sky suffused the faces of the brothers with angry color.

"We'll need more light," said the Earl as they pushed the furniture aside.

Without a word, Theo lit two branches of candles, set one on the mantleshelf and brought the other across to the table where he placed it well back; even so small an effort left him weak. He propped himself against the corner of the table and after a moment's consideration, laid his pistol close beside him. He had fenced with Staveley at Angelo's and knew him for a reckless opponent who hated to lose; in a situation like this he could be unpredictable.

Pilar had gone back to the settle, subdued now; filled with a quiet fatalism. She watched as the blades came up in a brief salute before engaging with a harsh scrape of steel on steel. There was something almost stupefying in the sound of hard breathing, the scuffing of stockinged feet across the boards, the constant clash of the blades.

Francis, as was to be expected, began aggressively, lunging recklessly as though he would finish his brother off in the least possible time; again and again Lord Ardwicke, by remaining cool under attack, counterparried, dropping his point under the oncoming blade, gathering it with a finger-light touch, holding it firmly on the forte of his own blade to sweep it out of danger. "You're good, Francis," he applauded, "but too impulsive!"

"Save your breath, brother," snapped Staveley, plunging into the attack once more.

Theo watched in admiration; he had heard Angelo speak of Ardwicke's skill, but he had never seen him in action. He was superb! But this was no friendly fencing bout; and Francis was strong as well as being twelve years younger. Sooner or later Ardwicke must tire; indeed he already seemed to be doing so.

Francis thought so, too—and lunged wildly. It seemed impossible for Lord Ardwicke to counter in time, but somehow his blade was there, parrying in a half-circle, and before Francis could recover, it was through and had ripped into his arm.

His sword clattered to the floor; the Earl stood back, his weapon still raised, his breathing labored.

Francis felt the blood running down his arm. He grinned savagely. "You'll have to finish me—it's the only way you'll stop me!"

There was a weary anguish in Lord Ardwicke's eyes. The point of his blade hovered and then it dropped. "I'll send for a surgeon," he said tonelessly, and turned away.

Francis Staveley's face was distorted with rage. "Goddamn you, brother Harry!" His voice rose in a tormented cry. "I'll not be beholden to you any longer!"

Before Theo realized what was in his mind, Francis had seized the pistol from the table and stood, spread-eagled with arm fully extended, aiming unerringly at Lord Ardwicke's back. In the instant before he pulled the trigger, Pilar's knife whistled through the air and sank home. Francis grunted, the pistol discharged harmlessly into the air, and he fell forward with a look of astonishment just as his brother spun around.

"Good God!" breathed Theo.

"I once told you," Pilar said shakily, "that the knife is faster than the gun. Is he dead?" Lord Ardwicke, kneeling beside his brother, nodded. He seemed dazed.

"He invited me to kill him a while back," she said. "And I could not do it!" And then, more pugnaciously, "But he should not have tried to murder you!"

"But . . . where did you get the knife?"

"It is mine. Always I carry it with me." She lifted her skirt to show a garter. They stared in awe, Theo with a gleam of outraged amusement.

"I had no idea you still clung to that barbaric weapon!"

"As well I did! Or my father would now be dead. You know he is my father?"

"Yes."

"God forgive me," groaned Lord Ardwicke. "You would have done better, child, to let Francis kill me."

"Oh, but what a nonsense!" Pilar ran across and took his shoulders in her strong, young hands. "How can you even think it? To shoot his own

brother in the back? *Madre de Dios!* For such
wickedness he deserved to die!"

"At all events, I owe you my life, for what it's
worth." he got slowly to his feet. "And Francis still
wins in the end!"

"How?" she demanded.

"Well, I can hardly hide what has happened. The
truth is bound to come out."

"I don't see why. Staveley's manservant never returned after delivering that note to you to your
rooms." Theo felt suddenly, appallingly tired. "On a
night of so much violence, one death is hardly going to raise a hue and cry. It will rank as the work
of an unknown assassin—and the truth, as you term
it . . ." He shrugged. ". . . well, who knows,
besides the three of us?"

"No one," he said slowly. "But I must tell Alice
. . . I must acknowledge Pilar as my lawful daughter! I owe her that much at least."

"You owe me nothing!" Pilar cried. "And I want
nothing from you!" She saw his look of hurt and
added in a softer voice, "Nothing but to know that
you are there. We will just be good friends."

"No! It won't do, child. I can't go on living a
lie—not now!"

"What is so different now? Would you lay the
burden of your guilt on shoulders less able to bear
it?" Pilar bent down and with a strong feeling of revulsion felt in Francis's waistcoat pocket and held up
the folded paper.

"My mother's marriage lines." She took them
across to the table and before he could stop her,
they were alight and becoming a curling pile of ash
in front of his eyes. "And if you say one word, we
will deny it, Theo and I. Sometimes," she pleaded,
"to say nothing is the hardest thing of all! But bet-

ter that, surely, than to salve your conscience at the price of your family's happiness."

She saw Theo put a hand to his head and sway slightly. At once she was at his side.

"Sorry," he muttered. "I have been little use, I fear."

"You should not have come, *mi esposo*," she told him severely. "But I am glad you did. Only now I must take you home."

Downstairs, the coachman still waited, though with the smoke in their nostrils the horses were growing panicky.

Soon Theo was leaning back with his eyes shut and his good arm around Pilar, who pressed very close to him. For a while neither spoke. Occasionally the coach was jolted, or swerved to avoid trouble, but the occupants cared little for the discomfort.

"Will Lord Ardwicke be all right, do you think, left there all alone?" Pilar asked at last.

"Stop worrying," murmured Theo. "He's a sensible man. I don't see him going to pieces. No doubt he'll arrange matters as honorably as he can for Staveley—and there, I trust, the affair will end."

There was a silence. Her voice came again, uncertainly.

"Was it very bad of me to kill Mr. Staveley?"

Theo's arm tightened. "No! It had to be. I was proud of you, *querida*—and impressed! I had no idea you were so proficient."

She wriggled closer to him. "I have never killed a man before," she explained. "And . . . I think perhaps I shall not do it ever again."

He dropped a kiss on the top of her head and said gravely, "That would be much the best thing.

A lady should not really go about with a knife strapped to her leg."

"No. And anyway," she observed practically, "I no longer have my knife."

Theo chuckled in the darkness. "Egad! We're a reprehensible pair! Lord knows what brand of offspring we shall produce!"

Pilar sat up with a squeak, remembering.

"Did you say something, my love?" he asked innocently.

Oh, no! She refused to tell him here, in this bumpy, noisy coach where she could not see his face. How surprised he would be!

"Tomorrow," she said. "I will tell you tomorrow." She laid her head back on his shoulder and her hand slid under his coat to lie warm against him. She was content.

Theo leaned his head back against the squab and closed his eyes, and though she could not see it, he was smiling. Tomorrow was soon enough, after all!

ABOUT THE AUTHOR

Sheila Walsh lives with her husband in Southport, Lancashire, England, and is the mother of two daughters. She began to think seriously about writing when a local writers' club was formed. After experimenting with short stories and plays, she completed her first Regency novel, THE GOLDEN SONGBIRD, which subsequently won her an award presented by the Romantic Novelists' Association in 1974. This title, as well as her other Regencies, MADALENA and THE SERGEANT MAJOR'S DAUGHTER, are available in Signet editions.

Ø

Big Bestsellers from SIGNET

☐ **EVIE'S ROMAN FORTUNE** by Joanna Bristol.
(#W8616—$1.50)*
☐ **FORGOTTEN LOVE** by Lynna Cooper. (#E8569—$1.75)*
☐ **BAYOU BRIDE** by Maxine Patrick. (#E8527—$1.75)*
☐ **THE SEVEN WITCHES** by George Macbeth.
(#E8597—$2.50)*
☐ **SONS OF FORTUNE** by Malcolm Macdonald.
(#E8595—$2.75)*
☐ **VALENTINA** by Evelyn Anthony. (#E8598—$2.25)+
☐ **LORD OF RAVENSLEY** by Constance Heaven.
(#E8460—$2.25)+
☐ **INSIDE MOVES** by Todd Walton. (#E8596—$2.25)*
☐ **LOVE ME TOMORROW** by Robert Rimmer.
(#E8385—$2.50)*
☐ **GLYNDA** by Susannah Leigh. (#E8548—$2.50)*
☐ **WINTER FIRE** by Susannah Leigh. (#E8011—$2.50)
☐ **WATCH FOR THE MORNING** by Elisabeth Macdonald.
(#E8550—$2.25)*
☐ **DECEMBER PASSION** by Mark Logan. (#J8551—$1.95)*
☐ **LEGEND** by Frank Sette. (#J8605—$1.95)*
☐ **BLACK DAWN** by Christopher Nicole. (#E8342—$2.25)*
☐ **MOONDRAGON** by Noel Vreeland Carter. (#J8555—$1.95)*
☐ **THE DEADLY PAYOFF** by Michel Clerc. (#J8553—$1.95)*
☐ **THE WINNOWING WINDS** by Ann Marlowe.
(#J8516—$1.95)*
☐ **THE MAN WITHOUT A NAME** by Martin Russell.
(#J8515—$1.95)+

* Price slightly higher in Canada.
* Not available in Canada.

Have You Read These Bestsellers from SIGNET?

☐ **SONG OF SOLOMON** by Toni Morrison. (#E8340—$2.50)*
☐ **MISTRESS OF OAKHURST** by Walter Reed Johnson.
(#J8253—$1.95)
☐ **RIDE THE BLUE RIBAND** by Rosalind Laker.
(#J8252—$1.95)*
☐ **KRAMER VS. KRAMER** by Avery Corman. (#E8282—$2.50)
☐ **RAPTURE'S MISTRESS** by Gimone Hall. (#E8422—$2.25)*
☐ **I, JUDAS** by Taylor Caldwell and Jess Stearn.
(#E8212—$2.50)
☐ **THE RAGING WINDS OF HEAVEN** by June Shiplett.
(#J8213—$1.95)*
☐ **THE TODAY SHOW** by Robert Metz. (#E8214—$2.25)
☐ **THE SWARM** by Arthur Herzog. (#E8079—$2.25)
☐ **I CAME TO THE HIGHLANDS** by Velda Johnston.
(#J8218—$1.95)
☐ **BLOCKBUSTER** by Stephen Barlay. (#E8111—$2.25)*
☐ **BALLET!** by Tom Murphy. (#E8112—$2.25)*
☐ **LOVING STRANGERS** by Jack Mayfield. (#J8216—$1.95)*
☐ **BORN TO WIN** by Muriel James and Dorothy Jongeward.
(#E8169—$2.50)*
☐ **ROGUE'S MISTRESS** by Constance Gluyas.
(#E8339—$2.25)
☐ **SAVAGE EDEN** by Constance Gluyas. (#E8338—$2.25)
☐ **WOMAN OF FURY** by Constance Gluyas. (#E8075—$2.25)*
☐ **CRAZY LOVE:** An Autobiographical Account of Marriage
and Madness by Phyllis Naylor. (#J8077—$1.95)
☐ **TWINS** by Bari Wood and Jack Geasland. (#E8015—$2.50)
☐ **THE RULING PASSION** by Shaun Herron. (#E8042—$2.25)

*Price slightly higher in Canada